DOCTOR, DOCTOR

Helen Godfrey Pyke

DOCTOR, DOCTOR

HELEN GODFREY PYKE

Review and Herald®
Publishing Association
Hagerstown, MD 21740

The author assumes full responsibility for the accuracy of all facts and
quotations as cited in this book.

This book was
Edited by Gerald Wheeler
Cover design by Helcio Deslandes
Cover illustration by Art Landerman
Typeset: 11/13 Palatino

PRINTED IN U.S.A.

98 97 96 95 94 93   10 9 8 7 6 5 4 3 2 1

Library of Congress Cataloging in Publication Data
Pyke, Helen Godfrey.
    Doctor, doctor / Helen Godfrey Pyke.
        p.   cm.
    I. Title.
PS3566.Y5D63   1993
813′.54—dc20   92-37123
                                                        CIP

ISBN 0-8280-0683-0

CHAPTER ONE

Doctor, doctor, can you tell
What will make poor Maggie well?
She is sick and about to die.
That will make poor Johnny cry.

John Hamilton dropped the patient record folder into the slot outside the examining room and went into his personal office two doors down the hall. This was the second cancer case he had seen today, and yet he felt an almost inhuman distance from the patient and her family. Instead of the medical data that he should be analyzing, he kept echoing that foolish rhyme he and his classmates used to chant at the country school when he was a kid. He wasn't even thinking about Maggie, although he had chanted that rhyme in his dreams often enough when Maggie was ill, his jumbled thoughts eddying around her face in frightening collages of bandages and operating rooms punctuated with church spires and open Bibles. Often enough he had thought he heard the voice of God pronouncing doom against her for taking him away from Him, and against him for going with her.

Automatically John locked the office door behind him, not that he expected a nurse to come in without knocking or a patient to inadvertently open the wrong door, but because he needed to place even greater distance between himself and the woman he had just seen. He sat down behind his desk and reached for the pitcher of ice water and the glass. Obedient to his professional instincts, he charted the glass of water—3:21—after he drank it. That made twelve glasses since 9:30 a.m. when he had come in.

"And I'm still thirsty," he said aloud, laying the pen beside the sheet on which he kept the record.

For the hundredth time he considered a urine test and rejected the thought.

Strange. Only a few months ago he could have come to the office overwhelmed with personal problems and yet thrown himself into the day's work, completely forgetting everything but his patients until the workday ended. He had survived every other personal crisis that way. Now he found himself unable to think professionally about a simple malignancy he would have to arrest. Now when Maggie was probably past danger. When Lora was sorting out her life again.

Even the urine test and what it might suggest was not the core problem. He knew that as certainly as he knew that slipped discs and gynecological complications were not at the center of Maggie's dilemma.

"Doctor, doctor, can you tell . . . ?"

"I could probably tell if I made myself face the issues," he muttered.

Enough now to admit that for all of them the problem was spiritual.

He started to pour himself another glass of water.

"I don't need more water," he said, putting the glass down again, considering his abnormal thirst—what it meant. "Not me, Lord," he prayed. "Not yet."

Unlocking the door, he stepped into the hall. So Mrs. Cavenaugh needed immediate surgery—though even that would probably be too late to save her. So? That was what his own life was all about—trying. A nurse was just emerging from the adjoining examination room, Mrs. Cavenaugh behind her. John answered the nurse's eye signals.

"Please come in and sit down, Mrs. Cavenaugh," he said, indicating the open door. He gestured to the empty chair, then walked around his desk and sat down himself.

Maggie was in the parking lot when he left the clinic an hour later.

"Tired?" she asked. "Too tired to stop at the dry cleaners on the way home?"

"No, not that tired." He set his briefcase behind the seat and got into the car, adjusting the backrest so he could recline. Fastening his seatbelt, he closed his eyes.

Even with them closed, John saw Maggie driving—much too fast through rush hour traffic, intent as she switched lanes, her crisp black pageboy framing the thinness of her face, her deep blue eyes darting from rearview mirror to side mirror to traffic lights and brakelights ahead. His wife drove aggressively, the way she lived, never waiting to see what opportunity might open up, always wedging into life's gaps . . .

John told himself to relax, but sleeping while Maggie was driving was out of the question. Still, if she drove, they would reach home a half hour sooner than if he did. He abhorred driving and hated the city.

"There are times I hate it too," Maggie often said when he talked about retiring early. "But you're used to the income. Besides, we'd be bored in a small town."

Whenever the pace became frenetic, John reminded himself about the financial advantages of city practice. It was true he enjoyed the security, but that wasn't what kept him from moving back to Blakeville the way he often dreamed of doing.

When John heard the turn signal ticking, he realized that Maggie was pulling in at the cleaners. He braced himself for the swing and the jolt over the curb.

"Five minutes," Maggie promised.

"Ummhumm," he murmured without opening his eyes.

The trouble was that there would be another Mrs. Cavenaugh tomorrow and the day after that. "At least I don't know the woman," he told himself. In Blakeville he would be facing Mrs. Remington or Leonard Adams with news like this. *Infinitely worse*, he thought. *Comforting thought!*

* * * *

Maggie opened the car door. The smell of dry-cleaning fluid swamped his senses—worse than anesthetics—as he clicked the seat to an upright position.

"Feel better?" she asked, flipping the key in the ignition and letting out the clutch abruptly so that the car bolted from the parking space into the stream of traffic.

"Any word from Lora?"

Approaching a red light, Maggie downshifted. "Rodnel is suing for primary custody. Lora phoned during her lunch break. She'll call again this evening after she talks with her lawyer."

Two hours later when Lora phoned, John had finished reading his *AMA Journal* and had flipped on the TV. Picking up the remote control, he turned down the volume when Maggie answered the phone, at first trying to overhear enough to follow the conversation, then deciding he would rather not guess but get the information all at once when they finished talking. As he reached for his Bible and Sabbath School Quarterly from the lamp table beside the chair, he remembered he'd missed yesterday's study. Today was Tuesday—not Monday, April 22.

As he had for the past 33 years, he methodically read the assigned Scriptures and the accompanying notes from the quarterly. Jotting the answers in the blanks, he briefly thought about the implications of the day's lesson. Then he placed the Bible on top of the quarterly that he had opened to the next day's assignment. As methodically as he had read the lesson, he reflected on his day at work and the problems facing his family. Still seated in his chair, his eyes closed, his head resting back as if he were taking a nap, he prayed. For 33 years this had been his one statement of who he insisted on being in opposition to Maggie's definition. Almost since the beginning of their marriage he had found it easier to be what she wanted him to be than to keep his connections with the church. He loved Maggie.

Sometimes in the night when she was asleep, when his own mind refused to let go of the day's events, he wondered if his love amounted to worship. Ever since they had been teens living next door on the graveled road at the edge of Blakeville, she had stood between him and every other consideration of life. He had never regretted what Maggie had cost him, yet at times he was aware of what life might have been if he had loved someone else instead. More often, though, he reminded himself that even the most ideal relationships were complicated, and even his friends who had stayed with the church had been through grief with their children. And he, of all people, knew that while those who lived right suffered less, illness and death still wiped out even deacon and elder, Pathfinder leader and Sabbath School teacher. *Doctors, too,* he thought now. *Not me. Not yet.*

Maggie was crying. He heard her blow her nose time after time. Her voice was unnaturally low when she replied to Lora's long explanation of her situation.

John pulled himself forward in the chair and got up. For a moment he hesitated in the doorway between the living room and the kitchen where Maggie sat, aching for her as she wept. Finally he went to her, sat down beside her, and put his arm around her. She shuddered involuntarily, then settled into the crook of his arm.

"Your Daddy wants to talk to you," she told their daughter.

He took the phone. "I can't understand the problem. You're the child's mother."

"It's not a foregone conclusion," Lora said, her voice controlled, tense. "Not any more. Even if we hadn't been married, a father can win custody—in cases where . . ."

"Where the mother is unfit?" he finished.

"Or where the father can provide a more stable home situation. Rodnel can, you know, Daddy. He's keeping the house, and Shelly is moving in as soon as the divorce is final and they can get married. She doesn't plan to work, and they will have a live-in housekeeper."

"Nice show of respectability!" John felt like laughing at the irony of the situation.

"It doesn't matter anymore," Lora protested, and then her voice broke.

"Baby. Oh, Baby!" John said huskily. "Can't we come? Let us come."

"No."

Maggie took the phone from him. "We'll be there by noon Saturday," she said with a firmness that seemed to admit to no argument. She murmured a few more words, then hung up.

* * * *

Arriving at her office at 10:00 a.m., a half hour earlier than usual, Maggie glanced through the faxed materials on her desk and rang for the secretary she shared with the two young accountants who worked for her. As usual, she found the challenges of her financial consultation business absorbing, almost relaxing. She worked until 2:00 p.m. when she left for a late lunch with her friend Corrine.

How many years had it been now that she and Corrine had routinely had lunch together on Thursdays? Since Corrine's husband Leighton had joined John's clinic in 1962. They had taken turns making lunch and staying home with the three children—Lora and Rick and Corrine's baby girl—while the others shopped all morning. Maggie smiled at how important saving the baby-sitting money had been for both of them then. When the kids started school, they had continued shopping and having lunch together, maybe taking in a matinee afterward.

My work's a blessing from any angle, Maggie thought as she parked at the restaurant. Corrine would be bored and lonely. Maggie felt guilty wishing she knew how to break away from this Thursday lunch ritual. *I don't need her today. I need two new clients on the verge of bankruptcy. That I could handle. I'd know all the right things to do, all the alternatives.*

Corrine would be melancholy—she saw it as part of her

duty as a widow. She would sigh and remember romantic tunes, sidewalk cafes in Madrid or Tornino, and golf scores.

"Madge, you look marvelous in green," Corrine said as Maggie took off her black linen coat.

Maggie laid the coat over a chair back and set her handbag on the chair. She liked the green dress herself.

"Christmas tree green in December, forest green in January, Kelly green in April. What's the matter, Madge? You look tired."

Sitting opposite her friend, Maggie reached for the menu.

"I've already ordered. Lunch is on me today. Is crab salad all right?"

"Fine."

"I always think of Charleston in April," Corrine said, looking out the window. "When Leighton was in residency at Bon Socours, I worked in a little dress shop on Glass Street. Greens were in fashion that spring. You remember 1958, Madge. Paris designers brought out the most fabulous silks in daffodil yellow and greens of every shade all the way into the blues—silks hanging in dramatic swags from the shoulders. Do you remember how those dresses moved? I used to love dancing in those dresses."

In 1958, Maggie thought, *we were still in New Orleans. John and I were fighting about dances. Yes, I remember those dresses. One in particular with a sheath skirt and the bodice fitted in the front, ballooned in back. John said if I wanted to dance, I'd have to go without him. And once I did just to prove I would.*

Corrine babbled about the love songs Perry Como sang and Fats Domino and piano music through open windows in Charleston's azalea-corridored spring. Maggie drifted through a dozen Aprils of her own—through a dozen pear-blossomed streets cordoned off for art shows—through a dozen art galleries that John loved. Her mind came to rest on a painting John had bought last month, brilliant with white and black and shafts of green and red.

I should ask Lora if Baldwin would ever make a green grand piano, she thought. *To go with that painting, to stand on the white carpet at the foot of the stairs, its brass feet and gleaming ivories crying out to my brass collections in their cases under the skylight.*

The waiter brought the crab salad and small triangular sandwiches. "I feel so much better about everything," Corrine said. "I wish you'd come with me. I've been trying to convince Lydia. It would do her good." Maggie realized she had lost the thread of what Corrine was saying somewhere after Charleston.

"Oh? Why should I go?"

"I know it's not the same for you because you still have John, but you may not always have him. I wish I had been better prepared for death and separation. It's wonderful to realize that Leighton isn't really gone after all."

I'm eating too fast, Maggie thought, deliberately holding her fork poised over the salad and chewing more slowly, trying to guess the drift of Corrine's remarks.

"Oh?" she repeated.

Corrine grasped her napkin with both hands almost as if she were praying. She gazed again out the window. "It's so comforting, Madge. I heard his voice for the first time last evening. At all the other meetings I just had this feeling that he was there, but last night I heard his voice as clearly as yours. 'I haven't gone away, darling,' he told me. 'I'm right here. I want you to go on being happy.'"

Maggie was getting the picture.

"It was wonderful." Corrine tended toward superlatives.

"I know Leighton would want you to be happy. Of course, he would," Maggie said. "Would you like dessert? Let me buy the dessert."

"No. Oh, no, I shouldn't," Corrine objected.

Maggie laughed outright. "Why shouldn't you? Didn't Leighton mean you should stop doing penance for outliving him?"

"Oh, Madge!" Corrine became serious, but finally smiled. "OK. Something frivolous. Something fattening." She studied Maggie a moment. "You're thinner, honey. Extra stress? At work? At home? How's Lora?"

Maggie resisted Corrine's invitation to confide. "I need another client. Cheesecake with fresh strawberries? I have too much time on my hands. I get bored."

Later as she drove to pick up John, Maggie replayed the conversation along with the plans she used to make for her husband every time she faced surgery.

If I died he'd have to marry someone right away to keep his life in order. John can't function without me. It's a basic fact. I would want him to be happy.

Would she like Leighton never go away but always be there, a spirit detached from back pain and migraines, wishing for nothing but John's happiness, sometimes influencing him for his own good—still managing for him? Or possibly more powerful as a spirit able to control the flow of influences around him—to shield him from all things threatening? With a shudder she remembered the red tie across the front of the white shirt in the shop window—red like a dagger, already guilty, its price discretely inconspicuous—but expensive, of course.

If I were a spirit, she thought, *I could stand between everything threatening and John*. Again she shuddered. *Or if he remarried, between him and happiness.*

She imagined herself a ghost, a fog of herself less substantial than tears or rain, almost like an incense odor or smoke—trying to demand his attention.

"Look, John, I'm still here. Everything will be all right."

"But he couldn't hold me," she said aloud. "And my ghostly hands—I could touch but not grasp."

Had Corrine really heard Leighton's voice? Or was her boredom its source? Was it her imagination—her memory?

Maggie knew what John would say. "The living know that they shall die, but the dead know not anything."

He had once told her he was quoting Solomon. Maggie wondered if possibly even Solomon had been wrong about some things.

* * * *

It was their fifth rest room stop on Saturday when Maggie realized what made her uneasy. At first she had thought that John was compulsively drinking Coke after Coke because of anxiety. Then she remembered the pattern. He was driving today, something he rarely did even on long trips.

John doesn't want to ask me to stop this often, she thought. *He remembers trips with his dad and the amputation.* As always, she was direct.

"Have you had a blood sugar test?" she asked when her husband returned to the car, another soft drink in his hand.

"No."

"Why not?"

He looked at the seatbelt latch, the ignition switch, the air conditioner controls, but not at her.

"Why not?" she repeated.

"I've been preoccupied."

Maggie reached to take the soft drink from him, then noticed it was sugar-free.

"You realize . . ." she began.

"Yes, I know."

"How long?"

"Maybe a year. I've adjusted my diet. I've been careful."

Maggie felt her breath entering her body cold, and freezing to the bottom of her lungs. "John, if this were me, evading an issue like this, you'd . . ."

"I know."

"You've had a urinalysis test done, of course."

"No."

"I'm calling from Lora's. Don't argue. You'll see Dr. Howell on Monday. I'll tell Sue to make the arrangements and cancel appointments with your patients. What are you thinking of, John? It's your life." She leaned toward him, placing her hand on his knee as he started the engine. "John?"

"Yes, I know."

* * * *

Lora closed the dishwasher and leaned against its front, allowing its hum, the vibrations it made, and the warmth of water splashing against its door to soak into her body. It was comforting in an odd way, almost like a human hand touching her.

CHAPTER ONE

I guess I'm not totally numb after all, she thought. She wiped the already spotless countertop with a damp cloth and prepared to mop the spotless floor.

I'm like Mom, she told herself. Finishing the floor, she then turned toward the bathroom where she continued her ritual, scouring an already gleaming tub and sink, using bowl cleaner, and finally mopping the floor.

Daddy used to smile about it—the way Mom went through all these motions every morning, even when we came back after being gone for the whole weekend. I think I know at least something of what compelled her.

After drying her hands, Lora applied a generous palmful of lotion, rubbing it in carefully around her knuckles and nails. *Bob always said that if I was anything, I was thorough. Thorough.*

"Nobody will ever be able to find fault with you, Lora," he used to repeat. "Whatever you set about doing, you abandon yourself to it with utter thoroughness." Those were his exact final words. And with that he had left her.

She looked at her hands. Still shapely, delicate, small, bare now of the several carefully chosen rings she usually wore. The sets of engagement and wedding bands she had abandoned now to her safety deposit box at the bank. Now she wore tasteful rings that nonetheless drew attention to her hands and the work she was doing with textiles and wallpapers, glassware and ceramics. Beautiful things that gave her such pleasure to touch. An almost human sensation of surrounding, enveloping, enhancing—creating an environment in which beautiful people could live and love each other. Lora leaned against the window casement and gave way to the feelings that had been building since she woke up at 4:00.

So here I am, she thought, *in an efficiency apartment with generic drapes and furniture, no glassware, no china, no books or memorabilia. No husband. No child. Mom and Daddy will be here by 11:00 a.m. No need to fix anything for lunch. Mom will bring everything ready to stick in the microwave.*

She had nothing left to clean, nothing to read, nothing to think about but what she had been trying to avoid. Lora went to the baby's room and sat down in the rocker facing the crib, staring at the quilt folded at the end and the Snoopy dog that Evyn hugged when she went to sleep. Slowly Lora began rocking, one toe tapping the floor, the other heel resting and rocking with her movements. When she had been a child she had sat on Daddy's lap, rocking with her cheek against his shirt, her arms reaching halfway around his body, listening while he hummed to her or kissed her hair. For all Rodnel's assertions, Evyn would not have memories like that. In spite of what he said, there would be day-cares and baby-sitters and hurried hugs between business deals. A stepmother who would get tired of being mother to a child left over from her husband's first love.

"Please, God," Lora prayed. But her prayer, as always, ended there. What else was there to say? What kind of questions could she ask a God she had walked away from? What kind of requests could she make? What kind of bargains?

So I'm beautiful and ambitious and thorough? Husbandless and childless. Great!

She remembered how she had felt at the age of 19 when she married Bob. Then she had believed that she was embarking on a wonderful romance a little like the one between her parents, full of delightful sharing and tenderness, complete commitment. Even though Bob was 20 and a college senior ready to return home to the family business in a few months, he hadn't been ready for that kind of a relationship. He was committed to fun on the weekends anywhere but at home, partying anywhere but at home. Dinner on weeknights anywhere but at home. Study until 1:00 in the morning at the university library.

"How can you be so single-minded, Lora?" he said one night when she asked him about a Saturday by themselves in the apartment and a quiet Saturday night with candles and soft music.

"Candles?" he had asked. "I'll get to smell a layer of bayberry over window spray and fabric softener?"

She remembered being with Carl. From the beginning

everything had been different. Although he was not yet 30 when they married, he was stable and settled in his legal career. Sober-minded, dedicated to his religion. She had converted to the Catholic Church for him. It seemed the reasonable thing to do, seemed so comfortable. They would build their marriage on solid values, raise children, contribute to the community, grow middle-aged and then old together. Except after four years there were still no children.

"Lora, I can't settle for a life without a child," Carl told her at last. "I want a divorce. I want a wife who can give me a family."

"But how do you know that I'm the one . . . ?" She had never finished the question. Suddenly she knew by the look in his eyes that somewhere, before they had met, he had reason to believe in his own fertility.

Carl's financial settlement had provided for her professional education. And she found wry comfort in remaining a devout Catholic while Carl abandoned his church for another divorcee who, friends reported, was noticeably pregnant at their wedding. He was taking no chances this time.

And she had married Rodnel because she was lonely and he was in love with her. Then unbelievable miracle! She was pregnant when they returned from their honeymoon.

"I'm delirious," she had cried into the phone, calling her mother with the news.

Now Evyn was 14 months old and Rodnel was in love with someone else. Someone not quite so beautiful, not quite so successful, not quite so—thorough.

Lora stopped rocking and got up. She went to the kitchen, where she began a major Sunday dinner with roast beef, chocolate pie with a raspberry glace and shaved chocolate over the whipped cream, potatoes to mash, two vegetables, a salad, and cloverleaf rolls that she planned to take from the oven at the stroke of 12:00 noon. Her mother's dinner would have to go into the refrigerator to be eaten as leftovers for the rest of the week. She was washing the last residue of radish tops and bell pepper seeds down the disposal when she heard her parents at the door.

CHAPTER TWO

As far as Rick Hamilton was concerned as he sat in the waiting room outside Bradley County Hospital's lab, the report from his doctor was the least of his worries. Rick had grown up in a medical family, surrounded by enough health information to swamp the "Queen Elizabeth." Since Dr. Wright had suggested the first set of tests, he had known that his run-down feeling was probably more than a low grade infection or overwork. He was just glad that all his insurance premiums were paid up—both health insurance and life insurance. With the coverage he had, it would take care of even the most extreme scenario he could imagine. If he was disabled for more than a year or died, the mortgage would automatically be paid off, and the few bills he owed were covered by an additional policy. As for the condition of his soul, that was all right too.

Rick thought about his situation at work where two men he had been training for several months were well able between them to take over his responsibilities. The company would not suffer from whatever time he would have to take off for surgery or . . .

But he was concerned about his wife, Beth, and their two small sons. Whatever was ahead for him was bound to disrupt the comfortable lifestyle they had all come to take for granted. The boys were used to having him at home every evening to play with them and cuddle them and tuck them in when they were ready to go to sleep. And Beth, while she professed bravery, never left the house without him after dark.

Every now and then Rick glanced up at the TV screen mounted on the opposite wall or at the open magazine spread across his knees, but mostly he reexamined his fingernails, their rough edges needing a file after the warehouse work he had done that morning.

"Mr. Hamilton," the nurse called from the door to his left. Dr. Wright met him in the hallway. Rick sensed he had bad news. "Leukemia," the doctor said after a lengthy discussion meant to prepare him for the report. "But possibly a more swiftly moving form than we usually encounter. You'll need more tests."

Rick nodded.

"You'll want to begin appropriate treatment immediately, of course."

Again Rick nodded. "Of course."

He listened for nearly 20 minutes to details of the current treatments and their possibility of success. Finally he said, "I'd like to discuss all this with my dad. He's a tumor specialist in Atlanta."

"Of course," the doctor replied.

That simple. Rick left the hospital and headed home across town. *I'll call while Beth fixes dinner*, he thought.

* * * *

In his study John Hamilton gripped the arm of his chair, rolling the chair back from his desk—then up against it, listening to his son's voice, hearing what Rick said, but somehow unable to deal with the information as facts.

"I wanted your opinion before deciding on the options my doctor gave me," Rick concluded.

John was surprised at the evenness of his own voice. "Let me discuss all this with some of my colleagues. I'll call you back tomorrow about noon."

"I'll be at work."

"Should you?"

"I might as well be."

"Does Beth know?" He heard Rick draw his breath in slowly. There was a pause. "I haven't told her yet. I went for tests as soon as I had reason to suspect anything was wrong. So I'm really in the early stages. I didn't want to alarm her with unlikely possibilities."

"But now she needs to know," John said. "Tell her. You need her support. You have no right to keep it from her."

"I'll tell her tonight."

"I'll tell your mother."

"And pray for us, Dad," Rick said, almost as if that was his real reason for calling. Setting the phone down, John rolled his chair away from the desk and slowly stood. He was on his way to his recliner, to his Bible and his usual prayer ritual, when he stopped short. *If ever I needed to get down on my knees and really pray, this is the time.* Kneeling beside his desk, he thought for some moments before his mind calmed enough to begin his prayer with the formality he thought it demanded.

"Almighty God," he said aloud. "Father in Heaven." He hesitated again. Then his voice broke in a half sob. "Dear Jesus! Oh, Dear Jesus!" That was how his mother had taught him to pray—the way he had taught Rick.

"I've become such a stranger with You. And now I feel like a fool crying to You like this. But I have no other place to go. For Rick's sake. His faithfulness should count for something. Oh, count it for something! Here I've failed You, but he's hung on. He's gone on without me, and where he's misunderstood what You expect of him, it's my fault."

His head resting on the backs of his hands, his hands pressing the edge of his desk, he knelt there, no longer praying but thinking that he had not bowed down like this before God since Rick was a child, since they had used to go to Sabbath School together, Rick in his three-year-old's suit and tie, repeating his memory verses in the car on the way to church, Rick kneeling with him beside his bed and praying in his innocence, "And make Mommy love You too so she can go to Sabbath School with Daddy and me."

CHAPTER TWO

But God never made Maggie do anything, and in the end, John reflected, he himself had given up trying to change her himself. It was easier to let her go on being herself, to accept the goodness she possessed as enough, to quit hoping for her to take down her guard and admit she needed God or grace.

So now we're all dying together, John thought. Well, dying in a sense. Lora, her heart broken time after time, and now possibly losing the child she had thought she would never bear—a heartbreak more profound because it was more basic, touching her womanhood as the other separations had not. And Rick. Possibly leaving them all, father and mother, wife and sons—lingering and suffering for who-could-guess-how-long, but inevitably leaving them forever. Dying. How could he admit to that word? *At least I'm not really dying, only learning to live with limitations that I've expected for years. I'll take care of myself. I'll not let this get out of hand the way . . .*

His hands, cut by the edge of the desk, grew numb. He remembered his father, living first with bandaged toes that would not heal, then those toes amputated—bandaged foot that would not heal, and then a stump and crutches, and finally death. Never coming to terms either with his diabetes or the other disease called sin.

At the mall Maggie Hamilton got off the escalator on the third level, walked swiftly to the end of the upper balcony over the fountain, and turned back toward the escalator at the opposite end. She jabbed the elevator button, thumped her right toe, and waited for the elevator door to open for her. Off on the second level, she circled the fast food plaza, and then returned to ground level.

"I'll not think," she murmured. "At least not until I've had more time to calm myself." *I'm walking,* she thought. *It's therapeutic. Same valuable exercise as always. Good for my back. Good for everything inside me. Whatever's left inside me. One of those surgeons took out something vital. Only I don't know which doctor or which operation. It must have been early. I've been a long time without a necessary part of me. All the remaining parts—compensate as they will—can't take care of . . . some vital function.*

Maggie was counting her steps, two feet per stride—half

21

mile. She hurried past the shop where she ordered all John's suits, noticing again the flash of one red tie against the grays and blacks and whites in the window.

"I'm going to start thinking," she told herself.

Back on the escalator she mentally turned the "on" switch. And exactly where she had forced her hysteria to stop, it resumed. The blood tests had been conclusive, but Dr. Howell had ordered others. To better define the progress of John's diabetes he said. How could John be so controlled? Of course, he had known for months even without tests, probably had expected it even when he was beginning his practice while his dad lived with them.

But he ate a piece of Lora's chocolate pie.

"John!"

On the third level again, Maggie found her inner counter ticking off her strides as her mind raced from one desperate thought to the next.

Cynthea's husband was dead. Corrine's husband was dead. Lydia had two dead husbands buried in the same cemetery. All widows in the past two years. Of her close friends, only Sally had a husband living and well. Maggie remembered her saying, "Madge, I'm almost embarrassed to have Matt. It seems almost obscene to be happy while Lydia is preoccupied with picking out a gravestone for Harry." And Maggie remembered her own reply, so glib at the time.

"At least I'll never have to be a widow. Sooner or later some doctor will slip up and remove my heart, and John will be done with worrying about me and my poor health. If it happens before Lydia finds another husband, do a little matchmaking, Sally. Lydia would take good care of John and the kids. What she needs is some grandchildren."

To be honest with herself, it wasn't exactly the threat of John's death that terrified her. It was the long-term illness, seeing his skin tones change, his vigor diminish.

John would take his injections, she decided, even without her to check up on him. And now that she considered it, he had actually adjusted his diet a long time ago. His professional commitment, his sense of responsibility for the family—these would force him to take care of himself. Maybe . . . Then she saw again her father-in-law growing steadily weaker, heavier, crippled, and mutilated by his disease. Not John! It must never happen to John! She would not allow it to destroy him. She wouldn't settle for his ghost hovering about. She would hold on to the real John.

When she had walked three miles, Maggie left the mall. In less than 20 minutes she was home.

* * * *

John heard the garage door open and then close. He ended his prayer abruptly and went to the kitchen entrance to meet her. During his career he had told hundreds of mothers their sons or daughters would die, but how would he tell his wife about Rick?

When Maggie thrust the door open, she nearly bowled him over. He stepped back.

"John!" she said, her eyes brilliant with surprise. She laid her purse on the counter and reached for him. And even as he held her, he felt her fingers sharp between his shoulder blades. She did not rest her face against his chest but forced him to look at her.

"John, we will not let diabetes destroy you. We'll control it."

"Yes, Maggie. Of course, we will. I recognize the importance . . ." He had forgotten about his session with Dr. Howell this morning. At the moment diabetes seemed a doltish enemy.

"Rick called," he said. And then he told her.

Maggie listened in silence. Finally she walked away from him and sat down at her place at the kitchen table, the place where she had sat for years while he ate her beautiful breakfasts. John moved mechanically to his own chair.

"Rick's doctors have suggested a bone marrow transplant along with chemotherapy, but he wants me to check with some of the people here about alternatives. There are alternatives, of course, Maggie. And several of the recent combinations are very promising."

"I know," she said so evenly that John struggled, off-balance again, not knowing what she was thinking.

"I'll call two or three clinics that specialize in leukemia in the morning," he said.

"Yes." Her hands were palms down at arm's length in front of her.

"Rick promised he would tell Beth tonight."

Maggie drew her hands back and pushed herself away from the table. "Don't ask me to think about Rick. Right now I'm thinking about you." She stood there, stiff, straight, her body as austere as the black lines of the cabinets against the white ceramic counter. John watched her breathe, shocked by what she had just said, but knowing it was the truth, knowing that between them existed their own kind of idolatry that shut out even their children when they came face-to-face with primal considerations.

Maggie was no longer beautiful, but John was always startled by the intensity of her face, the overwound tension of her body, even when she seemed to relax beside the pool or when they fished with Matt and Sally on the Gulf. Now as always, John was startled that Maggie was so thin, almost as thin as the girl of ten who had raced her bicycle beside his down the red dust road to school in Blakeville.

"I love you, Maggie," he said. And though she said nothing, he read in her eyes the truth that no matter how much he loved her, she loved him more. It was always that realization which subdued him.

"Have you eaten?"

"No," he admitted. He looked at the clock. An hour past the time Howell had set for his evening meal. Maggie opened the refrigerator.

* * * *

Rick stretched out on the bed beside his younger son, cradling the two-year-old's hand in his, crooning a half-hymn, half-lullaby the boys had learned in Sunday School, singing to them as he usually did after they said their prayers. He remembered his own father doing this with him almost until he began first grade, the one time of day he had Dad all to himself, the one place Mom never intruded. And he remembered the sense of loss he experienced after Dad set up his practice in Atlanta—when Dad gave it all up. First going to Sabbath School, then studying the lesson with him every night, finally even the prayers beside his bed. Once he had asked Lora about it. She said that she didn't remember any of that time. Nothing of church, no religious orientation at all, although she did remember the Bible beside Dad's chair in the den. They knew he read it but never saw him do it. In the years since he had married Beth, he had tried time and again to speak to Dad about having faith in God, about letting God lead . . . things like that. But conversations that touched on religion even peripherally turned off whatever closeness existed between the two of them at the moment, and Rick had come to praying silently when they talked about cars and real estate values that the commitment he felt toward Christ would somehow flow by some submerged channel—flow directly into his father's soul and nourish him.

His son beside him fell asleep, his tiny hand relaxing, releasing Rick's thumb. The damp fingers spread, yet hardly covered Rick's palm.

The child in the other bed stirred now and then if Rick paused in the endless lullaby, but finally he too stretched full length and rolled over, asleep.

Rick quit singing, lay still himself, praying. Then he rose and went to the kitchen. Beth had finished her chores and was waiting for him in the living room.

He sat down on the sofa, patting the cushion beside him.

"Come sit by me, Sweetheart. I have something I need to tell you."

Sitting there, holding her hand, he told her. At first her eyes betrayed fear and her hand trembled, but she listened and asked questions, listened to his inept reassurances, and asked more questions. No hysteria, no loss of control.

"We'll be all right," Beth said when he had no more to say. "God can handle leukemia." She paused. "But even if He chooses to let the worst happen, we still have Him."

"I wish my mother did. She'll have trouble coping."

"Your Dad, too."

Rick shook his head. "No. If anything, this will give Dad a better grip on his faith than he's had in years. It's just possible that God may be letting this happen to bring Dad back."

"I didn't know he was ever a Christian."

Rick gripped her hand. "I guess I never did tell you about how things were when I was a little kid—that I learned the really important things about God from my dad."

While the room cooled and the clock ticked and chimed, he sat there holding Beth's hand, telling her about the memories so deeply undergirding his personal faith that he had never spoken of them before. When he finished, his wife leaned to kiss him.

"For his sake, even dying would be a small price to pay," she whispered, tears dampening her cheeks.

"That's what I thought."

"Maybe your mom, too."

He pursed his lips. "Not Mom. She's made out of spring steel."

"Don't set limits on what God can do," Beth said.

CHAPTER THREE

S he had been counting her strides as usual, but after a while Maggie found herself repeating the nonsense rhyme they had used to chant on the playground, a "gaggle of girls," as the boys called them, two of them swinging a piece of clothesline and chanting while the others lined up and took turns running in and jumping the rope until they missed.

"Doctor, lawyer, merchant, chief,
    Rich man, poor man, beggar man, thief."

She was jumping, her hair slapping the back of her neck, her tennis shoes thumping the packed dirt of the playground. Her throat hurt. Her mouth was dry, but she was determined not to trip up on beggar man or thief.

"Yeh, ha! Yer gonna marry a doctor, Maggie!"

"Hey, Johnny! Too bad for you. Maggie's gonna marry a doctor!"

That was when she had made up her mind that John would be a doctor.

Their first year in high school she told him.

"John," she had said, "you ought to be a doctor. You're so smart."

"I've been thinking I'd like to be," he replied. And she was surprised.

They were in college before she realized that John had

been dreaming of becoming a missionary doctor. He had begun talking to her about the Bible when they studied at the corner table in the high school library.

"You'll never make an Adventist out of me," she told him countless times.

Her mother kept trying to get her to join the Baptist Church, and John quoted Bible texts trying to show her that what he believed was really based on solid evidence.

"Solid enough if you are going to accept the Bible as fact," Maggie conceded. "I'm not going to do that. John, you're smart enough to see through all those myths."

* * * *

At the center of the mall Maggie took the stairs instead of the escalator, sensing the increase in her heart rate as she neared the third level. *Now,* she thought, *John faces all this without anything but human resources. I took it all away from him. What did I give him in exchange for the faith he used to have?*

And Rick.

She had come at last to her son who, even when they were in the same room together, was a stranger.

Rick might be facing leukemia, but he and Beth were not left with human resources. They had God. As much as she had smiled at their childish Sunday-schoolishness, they had God now—now when they needed Him. Maggie shuddered, thinking again about her conversation with Corrine. Whatever tenuous comfort Corrine and her widowed friends found in that mumble-jumble measured out scant when compared to what her son and daughter-in-law had.

And then Maggie remembered the familiar picture of John in his recliner, his eyes closed, his Bible in his lap.

She stopped abruptly in front of a bake shop and stared at the displays of cookies.

"He's been praying!" she said.

The girl behind the counter stared back at her then shrugged. "So he's been praying," she said.

Maggie noticed the girl wore a cross on a thin chain around her neck. "My husband's been praying."

The girl looked away. "So?"

"So I'm the one who's left alone on the outside." She walked swiftly to the elevator, took it down, and rushed home instead of to her office.

* * * *

John had planned to go by radiology when he left surgery. Unexpectedly he met Howell in the corridor as he began rounds and told him about Rick's illness.

"Looks like you're getting hit with everything at once," the other doctor sympathized. "Fortunately your own situation need not be critical."

"That's what I tell my wife. Maggie sees only the worst ahead. My father died of diabetes. He lived with us the last two years. Multiple amputations until he finally called a halt above the knees."

Howell nodded. "Hmmm. No wonder your wife is upset. With memories that grim. Still, treatments have improved immeasurably."

"And Dad didn't follow the program unless he felt like it," John added. "We all talked to him about his weight even before we knew he was diabetic. Once he found out about the disease, he was pretty fatalistic, as if he might as well live how he wanted as long as he was on his way to the grave."

"Some people do react that way," Howell agreed. "Frankly, John, you're in good shape aside from the diabetes, and since you thoroughly understand the regimen and its importance, you should have few complications. Of course, as I told you in my office last week, you should probably cut back on your surgery schedule in order to reduce stress, stress being a major factor in controlling any chronic disease."

John reached out to shake Howell's hand. "I appreciate your advice, and I'll try to follow it."

"And about your son. We both know there are some very effective treatments available. Remember that."

A half hour later, still on rounds, John passed a room in which Howell stood beside a patient's bed, his head bowed.

John was part way down the hall before he realized what he had seen. Turning, he went back to look again. Howell still stood in the same posture, his eyes closed, obviously praying. When John finished seeing his own postoperative patients, he went to the chaplain's office.

"I haven't come to tell you all my problems," he said, shaking hands over the chaplain's desk, "but just to hear another human voice praying for me and my family. In a general way."

The chaplain looked at him strangely, John thought.

"God doesn't answer generic prayers," the man said. "God deals with specific issues whether we name them aloud or not." The chaplain smiled. "Of course, we can pray together." He walked around the desk and closed the door.

"Several members of my family have serious health complications," John explained briefly.

"I see." The chaplain knelt, and John knelt awkwardly beside him. "Eternal God, our Father, I ask You to consider Dr. Hamilton's family, each member individually. While he doesn't wish to burden me with details right now, You already know every detail intimately just as You know just what each of these dear one's needs for recovery and for peace of mind. I pray that You will supply the wisdom and peace each one needs and after that whatever physical healing that will lead to the eventual good You wish to bring about. We ask in the name of Jesus, our Saviour, Amen."

Even though he sensed that the chaplain waited for him to add a prayer of his own, John was still almost surprised at his own voice picking up the petition. "Heavenly Father, we all need healing in many ways. How can I ask You to heal us all? Yet, that's what I'm asking for, since I don't know how else to ask. I don't know anything else to do."

As he left the hospital, he felt a moment's embarrassment about his visit with the chaplain. It was the first time he had expressed a spiritual need to another person in more than 30 years. He had come to fear the cynicism he had never seen in a colleague's eyes but had always dreaded, the look he saw in Maggie's eyes during the first years of their marriage when he had tried to openly express his personal faith.

Seeing Howell pray at his patient's bedside had shattered that fundamental fear.

"I'm not the only doctor in this city who believes in God," he muttered to himself as he got into the cab to return to his office. Theatrics? Placebo effect? The thoughts crossed his mind, but he immediately rejected them. No, not Howell. He was not a man to play games. John felt a new calm settling his nerves.

Used to critical cases, John rarely saw a patient whose condition was less than serious. Death and the threat of death were almost hourly possibilities in his work. Yet, for all his exposure, he had never been able to steel himself against the personal pain of realizing that neither he nor any other medical specialist could prevent the inevitable advances of cancer once it had passed certain limits. His was always the position of outguessing the unseen enemy, continuing the fight even if he saw no reason to hope—on the chance that he might be wrong or that somehow he might head the invader off, corner it, and destroy it.

And he always hoped for divine intervention, if such a thing could be defined. Did not all patients survive because of divine intervention of some sort? Did he not himself arrive at home each night by some kind of divine protection through the bedlam of Atlanta's freeways?

Back at his clinic he made a quick inventory of the cases he needed to see before stepping into his private office. He knelt down beside his desk and named them, as yet persons unknown, but certainly in danger if their family physicians had made appointments with him.

"And Rick. Once more Rick, Father. Give him a doctor wiser than I am."

Maggie picked him up at 4:00 p.m. Rick called at 6:00.

"I've been praying," John told him. "And I went to see the hospital chaplain this morning."

He heard the intake of Rick's breath.

"That's good to hear. We're satisfied with whatever God allows to happen. Beth and I are. But I'm going to do everything I can to get well. I know God can take care of her and the boys if I have to leave them, but I don't want to leave them, Dad. I want to give them everything I can for as long as I can."

John's knuckles whitened as he gripped the telephone. "Of course, son."

Maggie took the phone and talked with Rick first, then with Beth. John watched her as she listened, for once silent.

"Would you like us to spend the weekend with you?" she finally asked.

"We're coming to Atlanta on Tuesday," Beth replied. "Do you know someone we might hire to stay at the house with the boys while I go with Rick when he has tests?"

* * * *

Lora walked once more through the Aimes house after the last delivery man had left. Except for potted plants, a fern beside the west entrance, and a Rex Begonia in front of the bay window in the dining room, everything was in place, ready for Don and Marie Aimes to move in with their three teen-aged children and their poodle.

I'm a year older than Marie Aimes, Lora thought, picking up her tweed jacket and her handbag from the chair in the foyer. *I could afford this house—I'd die in this house.*

She stopped only briefly at her office before picking Evyn up at day care. Lora had the child Thursday through Monday so that Rodnel and his love could have a long weekend to themselves.

"Stop thinking," she told herself as she opened the door and looked in on the roomful of toddlers.

"Hi, Evyn," she called.

The girl looked up when she heard her name but did not smile or come to her. Lora spoke to the woman in charge and went to kneel beside her child.

"Hi," she said again. Evyn smiled slowly, then looked at the day care worker.

"It's all right. Mommy's come for you."

Evyn looked confused, but in the car she smiled, reaching

32

CHAPTER THREE

to hug Lora as she buckled her in her car seat.

At home she let Evyn eat fish sticks with her fingers—and green peas and cooked carrots. Then she let her daughter hold her own cup of apple juice. She restrained herself and did not use the damp washcloth until Evyn had finished. Her child in her arms, she walked from the kitchen and turned the light out on the mess.

Lora sat on the edge of the bathtub watching Evyn bat her toy duck and a nearly empty shampoo bottle about in the water. And then, with her dressed in her sleeper, they sat on the bedroom floor playing "peepeye" with the corner of the comforter on Lora's bed.

Hours later, long after the baby slept in her crib, Lora lay awake. At last she took Evyn from the crib, still sleeping, and returned to her own bed. The child was not used to such cuddling and stretched herself flat on her stomach, grunting and sighing. Lora rested her hand on her daughter's back, caressing tentatively, careful not to awaken her.

After a while Lora remembered that she had left Evyn's half-full cup of milk on the kitchen cabinet. She had not washed the high chair or picked up the dropped peas and carrots. These details seemed unimportant now with the baby beside her.

In the morning she called day care.

"Evyn won't be in today. No, she's not sick."

She swept the kitchen while Evyn ate Cherrios.

Evyn sat on her lap behind the desk and then on the office floor.

They had lunch together in the park. When Evyn fell asleep in her car seat on the way back to the office, Lora parked on the sunny side of her building, rolled down the windows, and opened her briefcase. Why not? A pocket calculator could handle the math involved in the estimates she had promised to have ready by 3:00 p.m.

On Monday she phoned day care again.

"I'll bring Evyn by at 4:00 p.m. No, I just want her with me today."

After the weekend they were getting comfortable with each other again.

"Why don't you just move a crib into your office?" Lora's secretary suggested. "And toys. I would." She was a grandmother and had done a lot of juggling herself, she said, while her children were small.

"That might work," Lora conceded, "if you were the boss and I were your secretary. As it is, I'm out so much . . ."

She dropped Evyn off at day care minutes before Rodnel was supposed to pick her up.

The phone was ringing when she unlocked her apartment door. It was her mother. Lora told her about taking the baby to work.

"Has Rick called you?" Maggie asked.

"No."

A half hour later Lora sat beside her kitchen table, her hands folded almost as if she meant to pray.

Why Rick? Why someone so good? Why not a playboy like Bob or a skunk like Carl? Why couldn't Rodnel die suddenly of some terrible disease or at least be too ill to think about Evyn?

"God, you make no sense at all!" she said through clenched teeth.

* * * *

Maggie stood for several minutes in her kitchen doorway looking at John's new painting. She thought again of a green grand piano. Pianos—green or red or black. Would a piano ever—ever again— sing for them? Would John ever play it? And then she remembered. Her husband had been praying. In the three glass display cases her brass bowls, the 18th century wine cistern, and the wine funnels reflected the low sun shining in from the west windows. From where she stood, the room glowed, the painting lived like a palpable thought, pulsing from the wall. And Maggie reached one hand toward it, almost in supplication.

What is real? she thought. *This room and all I have put in it—all of John and me and our children? The purple ridge beyond*

34

those green hummocks dotted with rooftops—and the freeway and the hospital? Numbers on my clients' spreadsheets? Money in the bank? That painting?

"Is God real?" she whispered. And then, "He must be! He has to be! You're real, aren't You?"

She had prayed.

CHAPTER FOUR

Tuesday morning John faced two surgeries back to back. After hospital rounds he was scheduled to see patients in the office until 4:00 p.m., three of them more critically ill than Rick, he reminded himself.

"I'll stay here until Rick and Beth arrive," Maggie told him at breakfast. "Then I'll spend the morning with the boys myself. Corrine will come during the afternoon so I can be with Rick when he's finished with the tests."

John was nearly done with the second operation when he began to feel weak. "Will you take over?" he asked his colleague.

The other doctor's eyes questioned him over the white mask. "Of course."

John turned to a nurse standing at his elbow. "I feel . . . Dr. Howell is in . . ."

Because he did not lose consciousness, he realized that someone carried him from the operating room, that he was on a gurney moving down a hallway, that Dr. Howell was beside him, that someone gave him an injection.

"I didn't finish my breakfast," he heard himself say. His voice echoed back from the walls. "I felt nauseous."

"Is your wife at her office?" Dr. Howell asked.

CHAPTER FOUR

"Maggie's at home."

* * * *

*Small boys ought to be outdoors playing on a spring day like
this.* Maggie held Rick's younger son and led the other down
the foyer stairs to the recreation room. Toys kept for their
visits, snacks, milk—everything they needed to see them
through the morning—everything was here. And a phone.

It was 9:33 a.m.

In Blakeville on an April morning like this her grandmother always used to lay off rows and plant English peas
and lettuce and beets. On such an April morning her
grandmother's cabbages had bloomed like fist-sized silver-
green roses, dew-covered and glistening in the clean red soil.

"Mornin', Granny."

"Mornin', Maggie."

Bare feet in the clean red soil. Earthworms and wet grass
clippings. In Blakeville—long ago.

"Careful, Justin," Maggie said to the grandson already
careening across the carpeted floor on a three-wheeler. She
set Pete on his feet. He was not at all like Rick, she decided.
Much finer boned, darker. More urgent. She watched him
head for the toys and grasp a pickup truck. The way he took
it in both hands made her catch her breath. *He's like me*, she
thought.

Maggie called her office, dictated several letters for her
secretary to get in today's mail, phoned a real estate broker
about a client's overpriced house, contacted the bank and the
company that handled insurance on practically everything
she and John owned. She called Susan at John's office. Called
Lydia, and finally Corrine.

"I'll be over about noon," Corrine promised.

Maggie changed Peter's diaper, kneeling on the floor,
tugging the closures snug. He arched his back as she reached
under him to set him on his feet, threw his arms around her
neck.

"Wuv woo, Nam-ma," he said, kissing her.

Afterward Maggie contacted her office again with more

37

instructions for one of her accountants. While she explained to him the legal proceedings involving the documents he was currently entering into the computer, the light on the phone flashed.

"More later," she said. "I have an incoming call."

* * * *

John heard her footsteps approaching in the corridor. The door swung violently inward ahead of her.

"Hello, Maggie."

She looked at him, the alarm draining away and relief flooding her face.

"I'm glad you're all right."

"Just a dizzy spell because I failed to eat as many calories as I was supposed to for breakfast. I'm not used to balancing everything out with the insulin injections."

"Do you want me to take you home?"

"Yes."

It was as if he had somehow admitted a major defeat, but even as he thought about it as Maggie shot through traffic, John realized that he had no alternative.

* * * *

It was nearly 5:00 p.m. when Maggie returned to the house with Rick and Beth.

"Good news," Beth told John, settling herself beside him on the sofa. She caught her husband's eye signal about the boys and smiled back at him. "Rick's tests here show some encouraging signs." She squeezed John's hand, then stood up again. "Come with me, Justin, Pete. Let's see what you've been doing downstairs all day."

John followed Rick and Maggie to the kitchen where Maggie began immediately to prepare supper. He sat down across the table from Rick and sipped the soft drink Maggie had poured for him.

"So what's the prognosis?"

"Not bad," Rick replied. "At least not as bad as we

expected it to be." His explanation of the test results seemed plausible. John relaxed, decided that he would enjoy the evening with Rick and his family and save his worrying for later.

* * * *

As if they had all thought it simultaneously, the adults went downstairs with the boys as soon as the meal was finished. Their interest in the toys they had played with all day revived now that they had new spectators. John and Rick joined them while Beth and Maggie talked softly across the room.

"I'm too old to sit on the floor," John said after a while. He took a seat on the piano bench, nudging a small car with his toe now and then, sending it back to one boy or the other. Pete came to him and hugged his leg, giggling.

"Wuvs me," he said, trying to turn his grandfather around. John watched him as he reached to the keyboard, surprised that the keys were covered.

"Wuvs me," Pete repeated. "Wuvs me."

"Oh," John said, suddenly realizing what the child wanted. Pushing the lid back, he struck B G G F.

Nodding vigorously, Pete reached to touch the keys, startled that the sounds he made were the wrong ones. John let the child push his own hands back into position. Then he struck the notes again.

"Is that right?"

Pete nodded again.

Picking out the familiar melody with his right hand, John then began adding chords and arpeggios with his left. And Pete began to sing loudly and almost understandably. Justin came to climb up beside his grandfather on the piano bench and join in the song.

John glanced at Maggie. She and Beth had stopped talking and were smiling at each other, the way women do when warmly proud of their children. Rick joined the boys' singing.

"If I love Him, by and by,
  He will take me home on high.
  Yes, Jesus loves me.
  Yes, Jesus loves me.
  Yes, Jesus loves me.
  The Bible tells me so."

Without thinking where he had learned it, John went on to a modern addition to the old song, and after a few notes, Beth picked up with the words.

"Oh, how He loves you and me.
  Oh, how He loves you and me.
  He gave His life. What more could He give?
  Oh, how He loves you and me."

John continued playing—nondescript fragments of hymns and show tunes, 50s hits and Civil War songs, "Yankee Doodle" and "Skip to My Lou."

"It's 8:30 p.m.," Beth said finally.

"Hummm." Rick parked three toy trucks in a row next to the toy service station. "That means we had better start getting you fellas ready for bed."

The boys knew where everything was, including the guestroom where they slept when they came for weekends. John watched them scurrying for the bathroom where Beth had already stated running water in the tub. Rick nudged the three wheeler across the room with his foot and parked it beside the cars and trucks next to the fireplace.

"Give us about 15 minutes," he said, disappearing into the bedroom and closing the door.

John went to the phone and called the hospital.

"This is Dr. Hamilton. How's Mrs. Cartwright doing?"

"Everything's stable," the nurse reported.

When he hung up, he turned to Maggie. "Frankly, it was pretty scary. Doubtless, as Dr. Howell said, the extra anxiety compounded the situation."

"Just the same . . ." his wife began.

"I know. It's too risky to have something like that happen in the operating room. We'll do some regrouping . . ."

Maggie gripped his hand. "Regroup. Of course."

He could see through her eyes the mental patterns moving rapidly like a kaleidoscope in the hands of an impatient child. Already she had his practice reorganized, another internist hired, another surgeon.

"I'm not retiring."

"Of course not," she agreed.

"Or quitting surgery altogether."

"Of course not."

John was thinking aloud. "Maybe more diagnosis, more consultation."

"Fewer hours at the office," Maggie said decisively. "And fewer hours on rounds at the hospital."

He started to object.

"Yes, John. Dr. Howell said less stress."

How could he explain to her that working less would not really reduce his stress level? Maggie, of all people, should know that without being told. She became frantic herself when her work grew slack. Even ignoring finances, they both had to work to keep on living, Maggie in her way, he in his. He opened his mouth, ready to try to explain to her.

"Yes, John, I know."

"What did you tell Rick about this morning?"

"Nothing. Corrine came in while I was still on the phone with Dr. Howell. Rick has enough to think about."

* * * *

Hours later John still had not fallen asleep although he had pretended to be so that Maggie wouldn't worry. Now they lay side by side holding hands, acknowledging their wakefulness but not feeling like talking. Amidst the tumbling cycles of thought he realized that tonight he had not read his Bible, nor had he prayed, but he couldn't get up now with Maggie awake beside him. He thought of Pete and Justin singing with total confidence, just as their father used to sing "Jesus Loves Me." Perhaps, he thought, those hard times during Rick's childhood had laid a firm foundation on which he could build an adult faith. At least he would like to believe that was so. He thought about the Sabbath school lesson the week before—the story of the child Samuel—God speaking to him in the Tabernacle. Silently John began to pray, pouring out his own needs and Rick's and Lora's. And only when he paused did he realize that he had not mentioned either leukemia or diabetes, only the spiritual uncertainties that now seemed far more threatening. As he prayed, mental patterns shifted, and what had been nebulous spectral mountains became focused images of peaceful valleys bathed in stillness—almost heaven itself. One moment he was awake and praying. Then as if he had taken a physical step through a door into sleep, he was dreaming of heaven. He was reaching. God had his hand.

"Now you are the connection for Maggie," God said. "Hold fast to her hand, John, and I won't let go of you."

When John awoke at dawn, he still held Maggie's hand, but she had turned across his arm and fallen asleep with her head on his shoulder. As he released her fingers, his own hand felt numb from the all-night grip. Maggie flexed her fingers in her sleep and rested her hand on his arm. The clock in the hallway struck 6:00 a.m. before he slipped a pillow under her head and went to his chair in the family room off the kitchen. He would have a half hour before Maggie's alarm went off.

John remembered the sensation of himself being a link joining Maggie to God. For a few minutes he searched for a text he had read in one of Paul's epistles about an unbelieving husband or wife being sanctified by the believing spouse. Was that a promise? he wondered, or only a statement of a possibility? He couldn't recall the exact words. The same peace he had felt the night before blotted out the many problems he had meant to pray about. He wasn't even sure that he was praying—maybe only resting his case—trusting that because God knew all about everything already, it was safe just to accept the comfort and quiet he felt now. Switching off the lamp beside his chair, he sat looking into the darkness of the familiar room, at first seeing only the flashing numerals on the microwave in the kitchen, then his eyes adjusting until in the faint dawn he saw the outlines of chairs against the gray of the near window and gradually a pinkness in the sky. He got up and went to shave.

* * * *

Maggie was awake with the preliminary click that signaled that her alarm clock was about to ring. She turned it off and lay still for a moment, sensing that John's side of the bed was cool. She wondered how long he had slept, gripping her hand. Her wrist ached, and her fingers felt bruised. When he finished shaving, she was in the kitchen with breakfast started.

* * * *

For Rick this day meant continued tests and more waiting, more suggested treatments, and more choices. Hearing Beth stir, he touched her hair, and she opened her eyes.

"Good morning, Sweetheart," he said.

She smiled. "Your mom's up. I can hear her fixing breakfast. I'll run up and help her if you'll dress the boys."

Rick caressed her hair, a fluff of pale silver-gold on the pillow. "Mom may or may not be gracious about help."

"I know. I'll help her anyway."

Beth disappeared into the bathroom with an armful of clothes just as Pete kicked off his covers and rolled off the low bottom bunk. "Let's change your diaper," Rick suggested.

But the child was already out the door on his way to the stairs, his soaked disposable diaper weighing down the seat of his sleeper. "Wuv-woo, Nam-ma!" he shouted as he began his climb. Rick pulled on his jeans and a sweatshirt and followed, feeling very tired—more tired than yesterday.

CHAPTER FIVE

Maggie awoke Friday morning with a numbness in her right shoulder and a dull throbbing at the base of her skull on the right side. At least Rick and Beth and the boys were gone, she thought, as she considered a battle plan for dealing with another migraine. If she managed everything right, it should pass before Monday, but all next week her work would suffer. Slipping out of bed, she swallowed the headache tablets, then took a hot shower—as hot as she could stand it—directing the pressure spray on the back of her neck and spine.

By mid afternoon when she reached her spa, neuralgia and nausea had nearly overwhelmed her.

If this had happened Tuesday or even Wednesday—

The voices of the other women in the dressing rooms reverberated from the walls—echoed in the hollowness of her own head like thunder. She felt a familiar despicable shrewishness coming on, and she hated herself for allowing a headache to control her behavior the way it would.

* * * *

Lora arrived at the day-care just after 9:00 Friday morning.

"Do you or do you not wish to keep your child enrolled

here?" the director asked too politely when Lora explained that she wanted to take Evyn for the day. "This is a five-day-a-week program. We have a waiting list."

"If you are paid for five days, does it matter if my child is here or not?" Lora asked just as politely.

"The child's father provides us with a schedule each week specifying when you are to pick her up . . ."

Lora took a quick breath. "Come off it! Legally he has no authority to make that kind of stipulations at this point. Besides, I pay for your services. He doesn't."

"Of course," the woman capitulated, "if you wish to pay for five days a week . . . Just what arrangements would you like to make?"

* * * *

When Lora drove into Rick and Beth's yard after 2:00 p.m., she noticed that both Rick's work truck and the Toyota that Beth drove were in the driveway. The boys' cocker spaniel circled her car, its whole body awag in greeting. While Lora struggled with the buckle on Evyn's car seat and Evyn began to whimper, hardly awake after the five-hour drive, Beth opened the door.

Lora hugged her without speaking.

"The house is a mess," Beth apologized before they went inside. "We've been gone most of the week. I haven't even vacuumed."

"I didn't come to see your house."

Beth smiled. "I know. Rick's sleeping. The boys are in the backyard."

As she always was, Lora was surprised that a house as austere as this could seem so warm, so comfortable. She followed Beth through the dining room and kitchen to the deck where Justin and Pete were in the cattle business. Plastic fences and plastic cows tumbled around a red plastic barn with plenty of sand and twigs and rocks dumped in piles.

Lora set Evyn down while Beth pulled another deck chair into the shade of the house.

"I've been out here with them so Rick could get a little rest. He's so tired after all these examinations."

Although Lora wanted more than anything to see her brother immediately, she sat down beside her sister-in-law, both of them watching Evyn and Pete as they stood facing each other, obviously eager to be friends but uncertain how. Evyn's face grew increasingly solemn. Pete reminded Lora of the cocker spaniel, his small body charged with excitement. Suddenly he threw his arms around Evyn and kissed her loudly.

"Pete wuv-woo," he announced.

Beth laughed. "He used those very tactics on Grandma and Grandpa."

"And turned them both into melted jelly," Lora guessed.

With Justin supervising, the children began a scramble across the grass after something that Lora could not see.

"So what do Rick's doctors propose to do for him?" she asked.

"A bone transplant seems to be the most hopeful possibility," Beth answered. "His doctors plan to start checking members of the family for a tissue match."

"First? Don't they usually start with chemotherapy or radiation?"

"Rick has chronic myelogenous leukemia—CML."

"Which means?"

"CML doesn't respond well to either chemo or radiation . . ."

"Aren't they even going to try?"

"We don't have that kind of time."

Lora drew her breath in a gulp. "Isn't a sibling the best possibility? Could someone at the hospital check me yet this afternoon?" She had no idea what procedures would be necessary to get a sample nor how long it would take.

* * * *

John already knew his blood type matched Rick's and Maggie's did not. Getting the marrow sample would be a small matter and could be scheduled immediately, probably as early as Monday. He reached for the phone on his desk, then drew his hand back, realizing that he didn't need to consult with Dr. Howell to know that his donating bone marrow to Rick was out of the question. Lora. Her blood matched too. A second time he reached for the phone and dialed her office.

"Ms. Hamilton is out of town at least until Tuesday," the secretary informed him.

"This is Dr. Hamilton, her father. I need to reach her immediately."

"I'm sorry, Dr. Hamilton, but Lora did not leave information about her plans for the weekend. I'll tell her first thing Tuesday morning that you called."

Thanking the woman, John hung up. *Be rational*, he thought. *Even with CML a few days are not critical at this point. Rick's condition isn't that serious. But why waste any important time?*

* * * *

John knew Maggie had a migraine when he opened the door. The foyer and the living room, usually flooded with light, were like the interior of a medieval cathedral on a winter day, the floor to ceiling blinds closed flat. John drew the door shut carefully behind him and set his briefcase down without a sound. His wife would be in the bedroom with an ice pack on her head and a hot water bottle on her feet. She would want utter silence for the duration.

"Hello, Darling," Maggie said from the shadowy kitchen. She was at the table, a mug of tea cupped in her hands.

John sat down opposite her. "Is it still getting worse?"

"No." Pause. "I don't know." The edge to her voice meant that she was struggling for control. He wanted to reach out to her, but knew better than to touch her.

"No!" she exclaimed, seeing his hand move.

"Do you want me to turn down the bed? Get you some ice?"

"No, I'll just lie there and think, and thinking will only compound the problem." He saw her jaw muscles tensing, her mouth a straight line. "John, I can't handle all this. I keep telling myself I'm crisis-oriented, that I come into my own when I face disaster. Then I have to admit it's other people's problems that gear me up. I feel like all my mental machinery is shattered, rolling around like pebbles in a rock tumbler."

"Yes," John murmured.

Maggie set her mug down and half-turned from him.

"There are things that we can do," he said.

"But none of them will help."

"We don't know until we try."

"You're always trying," she snapped. "You make a living trying to save people you know will die anyway. It's a fraud, John, and you know it. How long does the average patient live after you operate? Six months? A year? Two or five years?"

He drew in his breath. "Some of them survive, Maggie, who wouldn't if I didn't try."

She stood, her body trembling. "Until they die of something else. That's where we're all going in the end, John—into boxes in the ground. Why prolong the pain? Why rake in the insurance payments and Medicare payments and tell the patients they will get better? It's immoral to get rich this way!"

"Any less moral than the fees you receive when you bail a client out of financial trouble just so he can get himself into another lawsuit?" He watched her walk away, her back straight, but her head drooping. "I'm sorry," he said as she turned. "I don't need to argue with you when you're feeling this way." As he stood across the room from her he wondered if there were any way he could tell her about how prayer had helped him cope during the past two weeks. "Maggie . . ."

When she walked stiffly back to him and leaned against him, he felt like a gladiator embracing a sword.

"I've found great comfort in . . ." John hesitated as Maggie pushed away.

"I don't want to hear about how you achieve serenity,"

she said almost in a whisper. "I can't stand a sermon the way I feel, John."

"Of course not."

She went to their bedroom then, and John to his study. *I have never needed her permission to pray*, he thought as he closed the door and locked it. *And God doesn't need her permission to listen.* He was ashamed of the bitter feelings that welled up in him. *Yes, I've seemed serene*, he thought. *But even Maggie sees only the outer layer of me. Inside I often seethe, possibly even more than she does.*

Sitting at his desk he stared at the calendar. *I'm a coward. That's the reason everyone thinks I'm so even-tempered. I don't want to make waves. If I weren't afraid of riding out a storm, I'd a lot of times say exactly how I feel, what I think.*

He clicked a ballpoint pen, retracting its point again and again, considering its shape and smoothness in his hand and the action of the spring inside it.

But then again, if I weren't afraid of riding out a storm, I'd be openly living for Christ, and if I did that, He'd be in control of my feelings . . .

"So here I am praying," he said as he knelt beside the desk. "Without Maggie's permission I'm praying for her. I know after all these years that You won't force her to do a thing she doesn't want to do, and maybe You can't even relieve her headache without her permission, but I'm asking You to Lord. I keep backing off from telling her that I've got to make some changes in the way I live, that I've got to match my doing to my believing. And I keep being more afraid of her disapproval than Yours. I'm not being fair with You, am I, Lord? I guess You're used to that by now. But somehow, I know because of the peace You've given me about Rick's troubles that You haven't turned Your back on me. You're still listening and still using me in some limited say. I'm trying to hold on to Maggie, to love her for myself and for You. And I'm trying to hold on to You at the same time. How am I supposed to do that?"

John remained on his knees for a long time, thinking of nothing else to say, his mind almost a blank—and yet not really calm. Finally he rose and went outdoors and walked around the back yard where the last of the tulips bloomed against the cedar fence. The sun was low in the west, almost to the treetops on the ridge.

Almost Sabbath, he thought, as he had done hundreds of times through the years. He leaned against the railing at the back door until it was nearly dark, then went inside, made himself a snack, and carried it downstairs to the recreation room. As he usually did when Maggie had a migraine, he settled in the spare room for the night.

She had still not stirred from their bedroom when John finished his breakfast the following morning. When he opened the door, he saw that she was still asleep. In a closet off the laundry room he found a white shirt and clean underwear and went back downstairs to shave and shower and dress. He was in the car before he admitted to himself that he meant to go to church. Although he often passed an Adventist church on his way to the hospital, he had never noticed when services began. When he pulled into the parking lot at 9:00 a.m., there were only three cars there. Turning around in the parking lot, he headed back onto the street and drove in wide circles around the community for 20 minutes before returning. While he would draw too much attention by arriving late, he certainly did not want to stand in the foyer talking to a deacon or the receptionist until the members arrived.

Certainly this was not Blakeville, and of course, thirty-some years had passed since he had been to church, yet he was unprepared for what he saw when he entered. Most of the men and women seated in the sanctuary might have been members of the hospital board, successful-looking people. The look of success didn't bother him. The classy hairstyles, the makeup, and the jewelry did. He sat down, waiting for something to happen inside him, telling him he had come home. Nothing did. Not until the music began. Although Sabbath school proceeded less formally even than the Blakeville one had in his childhood, and although the organist and pianist were better trained, the songs were the same he had grown up with—Fanny Crosby, Beldon, and deFlutier, songs that had been in the old red *Christ in Song* his mother had carried with her to church. When a young man prayed after a Scripture reading, John smiled.

How could anyone so young speak even to God in such archaic terms? Even the Adventist cliches made him feel he had come home.

He was kneeling at the throne of grace.

He was praying for missionaries in foreign lands.

He was praying for the sick and afflicted, the poor and the needy.

He asked for forgiveness for his sins and mistakes, making a distinction between them.

And while John smiled at the set language, he knew the young man meant every word he said just as generations of earlier Adventists had meant what they prayed for. John arose from his knees feeling that all of the bases had been covered. Until the children came in from their classes after Sabbath school, he did not realize how cosmopolitan the church had become. Although he had expected some Blacks in the congregation, he had not foreseen the number of Hispanics and Asians or the accentless speech he heard from the pulpit. What had happened to their southern accent?

The pastor was certainly not a southerner. John remembered the word the hospital chaplain had used to describe his request for prayer. Generic. Could there be such a thing as a "generic" Seventh-day Adventist, without a home church label pinned to his lapel, maybe even totally without a hometown and regional accent because he had been on the move all his life from one Adventist point of service to another?

I might have done that, John thought, musing on his boyhood dreams of seeing the world as a missionary doctor. *Instead I've spent my whole life in Georgia. Not a bad place to spend a lifetime. Plenty of work to do right here. Plenty of heathen in Atlanta. Plenty of people dying.*

"Praise God from Whom all blessings flow.

Praise Him all creatures here below.

51

Praise Him above ye heavenly hosts.
Praise Father, Son, and Holy Ghost."
What had they done to the time signature, the tempo?

The sermon was more polished than those he had grown up with, but basically the theology was the same. Or, he reflected, if the theology had changed, his own ideas had moved in step because he had been studying the lesson quarterly all this time.

"I'm from Blakeville," John said when the pastor shook his hand in the foyer.

"Visit us again if you're back in Atlanta," the minister said.

"I may."

* * * *

Maggie was vacuuming the living room when he reached home. The house dazzled with all the blinds open.

"You're feeling better," he said.

She nodded and continued her work. "There's a salad plate for you in the fridge," she told him above the noise.

John took off his coat and tie and came back to the kitchen just as his wife turned off the vacuum and began putting it away. He got the salad she had prepared and sat down.

"I'll eat with you," she offered.

"I'm glad you didn't have to suffer through a three-day siege."

She poured herself a glass of iced tea. "I woke up at 8:40 a.m. when you started the car. I felt wonderful. Still do. Not even a drugged hangover from the pain prescription. I know the cleaning woman is coming on Monday, but I felt like doing some housework myself. Where did you go?"

"I drove around a bit," John began. He swallowed a mouthful of deviled egg. "I went to church."

"Oh." Maggie sounded neither surprised nor upset. She was silent for a while, eating as if she were quite hungry. "You didn't forget your insulin this morning?" she said at last. "Your things were in the cabinet in our bathroom."

"I had some in my study."

"I can't get over the headache leaving like it did." Maggie began clearing the table, and John took his own plates to the dish washer. "I was prepared for the usual devastating ordeal."

"Just be thankful," John replied. "Are you ready for a sermon now?"

"No, John, I'm not."

* * * *

Matt called that evening, inviting them to play golf with him and Sally on Sunday afternoon.

"I know you're feeling depressed about Rick's illness," he said. "But on the other hand, you need to get outdoors a bit to break some of the tension."

They had gone half away around the golf course when John mentioned the bone marrow transplant to Matt.

"Could you be a match?" Matt inquired.

"Very likely."

Maggie turned suddenly from studying her shot. "No, John. You can't."

"Why can't he?" Matt asked in surprise. "He's in good shape. It's not life-threatening to donate marrow, Maggie."

"John's diabetic. Nobody's cutting John's legs for any reason. Not even to save Rick."

Matt turned to John. "Really? Since when?"

"It was in my genes when I was born," John replied, trying to shift the conversation to a lighter mood. But even as he spoke he thought of his father, and he knew his voice ended in an almost flat despair. "Lora has the same blood type. It's very possible she could be a donor."

"Or one of the boys," Matt suggested.

"Oh, they're much too young," Maggie objected.

Matt leaned on his golf club. "It doesn't take much, Maggie. I've heard of experiments using fetal tissue for other transplants. Why not from one of Rick's sons?"

CHAPTER SIX

On Thursday John considered what he would do on the coming Saturday. As he had lain awake the night before, he had decided that from now on he would at least attend church, and he would make no excuses to Maggie or to anyone else. His work, of course, posed no problems of conscience, for unless a patient's life was at risk, he was never scheduled for weekend surgery, and only when a patient needed careful monitoring did he make hospital rounds then. Social engagements might pose some conflict, but he was ready now to openly state his position as a Christian and as a Seventh-day Adventist. At least that was what he had decided. However, carrying out the decision seemed more complex. For one thing, he was not yet ready to establish the close congregational ties that would automatically develop if he began attending a particular church regularly. Returning to the church he had visited the previous week would be awkward after he had led the pastor to believe he still lived in Blakeville.

Before seeing his first patient on Thursday, John looked in the phone book for listings of Seventh-day Adventist churches in the Atlanta area, and photocopied the page.

* * * *

Maggie arrived at the restaurant before Corrine. Although she was not hungry, she thought she would order a ham salad and hard rolls. When she noticed that the menu listed fresh asparagus, she changed her mind.

"What have you heard from Rick?" Corrine asked as she sat down.

Maggie stiffened. "Nothing. Absolutely nothing."

"Isn't anybody doing anything?" Corrine nodded to the waitress that they were ready to order.

"Something, I suppose," Maggie admitted. "But nothing that seems likely to produce results. Lora's bone marrow doesn't match. Beth says they may check Justin and Pete next week."

"How awful! Madge, that's awful."

"Not really," Maggie corrected her. "But at least bad. It seems cruel to put a small child through an experience like that, but when you think of the alternatives . . ."

"I suppose so," Corrine conceded.

* * * *

Maggie had completed everything she had scheduled for herself at the office by noon on Friday, then stopped by a supermarket on the way home, mentally outlining the meals for the weekend. She was almost certain that John planned to attend church again tomorrow. Perhaps she would make a potato salad and a carousel of raw vegetables, maybe suggest a drive in the country after they ate.

The phone rang while her potatoes were boiling.

"Mom, I may win custody," Lora said. "Rodnel has been drinking. A lot of people know about it. My lawyer says this will make a good case."

"I'm so glad. What about his girlfriend? Is she still eager to play stepmother?"

Lora sighed. "She says she is. But then, she's drinking too, so . . ."

"Everything will work out. You have to believe that."

"I wish I could, but after what's happened to Rick, I don't have much faith in anything, including God. I think it's pretty much up to us to figure out things for ourselves and do whatever we can to make the best of what happens."

* * * *

Later, cutting up the still warm potatoes, Maggie thought to herself that even a month ago she would have agreed with Lora. Now she sensed something else going on, something under the surface of life or possibly above it. It was something that had to do with the fact that John prayed. She knew that intuitively. After covering the potato salad and putting it in the refrigerator, she went to the family room and sat down in John's chair. For several minutes she stared at John's Bible, an object she had lived with for 35 years but had never opened. Finally she lifted it and reached for the booklet that always lay under it.

When she opened the quarterly, she saw that it consisted of questions and blanks for answers. On one line in John's loose scrawl were the words, "Speak, Lord, for thy servant heareth."

The power of those words struck her as almost frightening. And then she remembered her own conviction more than a week ago and her admission, "You are real, aren't you, God?"

Because she didn't know where to begin in the Bible, she turned the pages of the small booklet at random, reading a line here, a passage there.

The topic of obedience caught her eye. John hadn't studied this far yet because the lesson dates were still three weeks in the future. And yet, all the years he had been reading the Bible he had probably come upon these words before. Was John ready to do what for so long he had believed was right? How would her own life change if he did? How much of what he had always believed would she be willing to accept if she could see clearly that . . .

Maggie remembered how threatened she had felt when first Rick and then Lora rejected her pragmatic views and became Christians.

"It's almost as if you thought I was becoming a Hindu,"

her daughter had said when they argued about her converting to the Catholic Church.

"It is almost as bad," Maggie had replied. "It's all so primitive, so filled with superstition and magic. How can you intelligently consider . . . ?"

"Does it ever occur to you, Mom, that a person needs a little magic in life just to survive?" Lora had countered.

And now she was disillusioned with the magic, the supernatural solutions she had once thought were available to her. Had she become more intelligent . . . or less wise? Maggie was not sure. For Rick, at least, religion had worked. In his marriage it had provided the influence that created a harmony that Maggie realized had never existed for her and John despite their deep love for each other. Where Rick had found God, Maggie had never discovered. He had met Beth in college after he joined his church. They had married before he finished his junior year, and he had decided on a career in industry. Maggie was never sure whether to blame religion or Beth for dampening Rick's ambitions. She had always hoped he would become an electrical engineer. Instead he had become a technician and then a supervisor, but still not a professional person.

But happier, she admitted now, than he would likely have been had he finished engineering. Happier than she or John had ever been. Even now when there was a very strong possibility that he was going to die. His happiness wasn't the result of his career choice, she decided, but of his commitment to a Christian life. Was it magic or something else?

Something else. The something else she kept coming back to when she thought about John's secret spiritual existence. She had always believed that knowledge gave power—in science, in industry, in business, in any endeavor. Why not in spiritual things? Evidently Rick had a good grip on that knowledge and power, and John almost had it. She turned the Bible over and over. No, it was not a magical object that could work spells for her, but she did feel convicted that inside its covers was the knowledge that could give her power, too, and right now she needed that power, wanted it more than she had ever desired anything else in her life. But she was not ready to become a Seventh-day Adventist or to go to church—any church.

"Will You deal with me on my own terms, God?" she asked aloud.

Then she opened the Bible to the first page of text. "In the beginning God created the heavens and the earth . . ." She would not wallow in all that creation myth although she was sure that some of it had symbolic meaning that she might want to think about later. Instead she turned to the Gospel of John because she had heard more about it than about any other part of the Bible.

"In the beginning was the Word . . ." John had underlined several verses. "The Word was with God, and the Word was God. All things were made by him, and without him was not anything made that was made."

This was weird—whole phrases echoing from the first page of the Bible into a passage written hundreds of years later. In the margin John had written, very neatly for him, "Revelation 14:7." After some searching, she found it.

"And worship him that made heaven and earth, the sea, and the fountains of waters." Beside the text was another of John's marginal notes: "Exodus 20:8-11."

When she located that reference, she recognized immediately that it was part of the Ten Commandments that she had memorized in Sunday school as a child. John had underlined "For in six days the Lord made heaven and earth, the sea, and the fountains of waters." Another echo.

"All right, God," she said. "On whose terms? Yours? If I'm going to get what I want out of this Book, am I going to have to junk my own prejudices? My superstitions?" She stared at the page, her eyes not focusing on anything written there, but it was as if every line answered her question, "Yes."

"I don't know whether I can," she said aloud. She laid the Bible back where she had found it, picked her handbag up from the kitchen desk, and took out her keys. She would have to think a lot more, but now she had to pick John up at his office.

CHAPTER SIX

* * * *

Six Black young men from the academy sang for Sabbath school in the church John attended the next day. They presented some rather modern stuff he had never heard before, songs with intricate, delightful harmony and even more delightful dissonances that pulled at questions deep in the soul. But they finished with a Spiritual that he did know.

"Lord, I want to be a Christian in-a my heart,
  in-a my heart,
 Lord, I want to be a Christian in-a my heart.
 In-a my heart, In-a my heart,
  Lord, I want to be a Christian in-a my heart."

John found himself mentally singing those words and the following stanza, "Lord, I want to be like Jesus," as he drove home.

* * * *

While Maggie cleared up after their lunch, he went downstairs to the piano in the recreation room. He knew without looking that there were no books containing hymns, only the various instructional books Rick and Lora had practiced from. His own collection of classical pieces was in a box in some closet. Any hymnbooks he had ever purchased had long since disappeared. But he opened the cover over the keyboard and let his fingers follow long-ago memorized paths, reproducing songs that he had been silently singing in his head all the years that he had lived there. If Maggie objected, she did not come down and tell him so, and since she did not, he continued to play for more than an hour.

Upstairs, Maggie sensed the power in what John played, the confidence, the peace. She sat down with a magazine near the window with its view of almost rural fields and woodlands and the distant ridge. Laying the magazine aside, she gazed at the early May sky which was cloudless today, and at her own small rose garden, just now in first bloom. She supposed the tunes John played had words, yet she couldn't remember hearing any of them sung. Looking at all the green outdoors, she thought again of the green piano she had envisioned in the living room and smiled to herself. It was good to hear John playing again. For a moment she briefly considered going for a drive in the country, but dismissed the thought. She felt something unwinding, loosening inside her. Taking off her shoes, she stretched out on the sofa, consciously relaxing first her toes, then her ankles, her calves, her knees, her thighs—an exercise she often practiced at night in an effort to go to sleep. When she began to concentrate on relaxing her spine, she laughed at herself.

This is ridiculous, she thought. *I'm already as limp as a sleeping cat.*

John thought of a sleeping cat too when he entered the room later. *A very small, elegant cat, maybe Maltese*, he decided, *half curled, its chin on its paws.* Sitting on the end of the sofa, he took her feet in his lap. The sun was an hour above the horizon when Maggie stirred. He reached for her hand.

"Good morning, Darling," she said, and he felt the charge of tension return to her body. "I've slept too long. What time is it?"

John looked at his watch. "Nearly 7:00. Does it matter?"

"Have you eaten?"

"No."

"John!"

As he followed her to the kitchen, knowing what help she would accept and what would irritate her, he wanted to tell Maggie it had been a good day, a wonderful day. He wanted to ask her if she had not experienced at least a little of the Sabbath rest that he had had in letting go of burdens, but he said nothing as he set the table for two.

* * * *

Lora spent half of Sunday morning playing games with Evyn on her own unmade bed. Finally she bathed her, dressed her, and stripped the sheets for washing, shaking out the bread crumbs and dry cereal into the bathtub. Evyn had discovered how to open the drawer of the small chest beside the bed. She stood there opening and closing it, studying its response to her efforts. Even after their relaxed play, Lora thought, Evyn was solemn, as if intent on finding what made things happen, as if she was already trying to take some control over her surroundings.

Or am I transferring my own feelings to my baby? Lora asked herself.

When the child caught her fingers in the drawer, she screamed. Lora took her up and kissed the fingers, trying to cuddle and comfort, but feeling awkward. Evyn squirmed free and returned to the drawer, pulling it out again and resolutely shoving it closed. *What's going on in her head?* Lora wondered. *I don't even know my own baby.*

Remembering Peter's confiding, outgoing laughter, she longed for Evyn to look at her that way, to say, "Wuv-woo," with the same certainty. *What would I have to do to achieve that?* she asked herself. Something Rick and Beth were obviously doing for their boys. *Spending rare time together? Touching? Listening? Paying attention?* The washer shifted from spin to rinse. Lora dressed in jeans and a tee shirt.

"Want to go outside, Evyn?"

* * * *

For Beth the morning had been an ordeal. Rick had insisted on going to church even though she felt sure he would be better off resting at home. The boys had been fidgeting, and Justin's teacher had called Beth from her own Sunday school class to settle him down. Afterward she had heard nothing of the sermon because it took all her attention to occupy Justin and Pete and keep them quiet. She was grateful that they had finally gone to sleep after their lunch.

"Sorry it was such a hassle," Rick said when she came to sit beside him in the living room. "But I needed all the support I could get, and I needed to go to church."

"I know. It's just that . . ."

"Sorry I couldn't help you more with the boys today."

"Don't be sorry. If you had helped me with the boys, you wouldn't have had time to get the blessing you went for."

"Meaning? That you came home without a blessing?"

"Umhum."

"Sweetheart, you give an awful lot without expecting much for yourself."

"I'm glad you noticed," Beth said, then instantly felt ashamed of herself. "I didn't mean that, Rick."

"I feel that way sometimes too," he admitted. "At work quite often, and even here at home once in a while. Is it so bad to enjoy a thank-you? Even the Lord appreciates appreciation."

Beth smiled and settled her head on his shoulder.

"I'm so glad I have you," she said. And suddenly an overwhelming realization of what her life would be if she lost him began to grip her. *I'm sorry, Lord*, she thought, *but even You won't be enough to fill his place if he dies. Am I rebelling?* she asked herself. *Lord, I'm not rebelling against Your will. How can it be Your will for Rick to die? He's going to get well or at least survive. At least let him survive.*

Rick sensed her feelings and rubbed her shoulders, his lips against her hair. "Are you still sure you want them to go ahead with the bone marrow test on the boys tomorrow?"

"Yes."

"Even though the test will be painful."

"Losing their daddy would be a lot more painful."

CHAPTER SEVEN

A s John stepped into the hall after seeing a patient the receptionist told him that Rick was on the phone.

"I'll talk to him now," John said, handing the nurse the folder he held in his hand. Stepping into his office, he closed the door behind him.

"Justin's sample showed the wrong type, but Pete's matched," Rick said. "Since he isn't 2 yet, I'd like to wait a little longer before putting him through surgery. What do you think, Dad?"

John thought of his small grandson's trusting exuberance. "I know how you feel, but since he will have to be the donor, sooner seems better to me than later. He will remember less of the trauma. You'll have a better chance of recovery. What does your doctor think?"

Rick cleared his throat. "He's with you. Is it all right if I have him call you to talk about the surgery? I'd feel more comfortable, Dad, if you were briefed and were satisfied that we're making the right decisions."

Rick's specialist called in less than an hour.

"Delay will only diminish possibility of success," he said. "I will be honest with you, Dr. Hamilton, as I know you wish me to be. Your son's situation is more grave than he imagines. I have tried to be positive in my discussions of

CML with him and his wife, but I have not concealed the seriousness of his condition either. They choose to believe that medicine can work miracles."

"I'm sure," John replied, "that Rick and Beth understand your professional limitations, but they're naturally hopeful."

"Encourage them to go ahead immediately," the doctor said. "We'll need every advantage that time can give us."

"I will," John assured him.

The surgery would take place in Atlanta for several reasons. Its hospitals offered more sophisticated technology than was available in Bradley County. Both Rick and Beth expressed faith in the surgeons John had recommended, and of course, having the house there as headquarters for caring for Justin and Pete was a major consideration. The operation was scheduled for early June.

"I've told Pete what's to be done," Rick told his father after the decision was made. "He's pleased to be able to help me get well."

"Was it wise to tell him?" Maggie worried. "Won't he become anxious about the whole thing with all this time to think about it?"

"Maybe not," John said. "I hope not."

* * * *

When John had an appointment with him, Dr. Howell expressed his encouragement with the progress they had made in stabilizing the diabetes.

"I've limited myself to one surgery at a time and only three days per week," John told him. "And I have a young man joining my clinic when he finishes his residency in July. I'm trying to be realistic."

"You're moving in the right direction," Dr. Howell commented. "But even if you are pressed with emergencies, you probably should cut back still more before July. Also you need more mild exercise on a daily basis instead of two or three days of vigorous exercise each week as you have had in the past. You say you are experiencing less tension?"

John leaned back in his chair. "I'm almost embarrassed to

tell you this, Dr. Howell, but I've been a Seventh-day Adventist in hiding for more than 30 years. I was afraid—I don't know what I was afraid of. Seeing you praying with a patient a few weeks ago at the hospital gave me the courage to begin practicing my convictions. I've discovered that I was receiving only minimal benefits from the kind of religion I had settled for."

"Good thinking," Howell exclaimed. "And how is your son? I know you've been praying for him, and so have I."

* * * *

As Atlanta's summer set in during mid-May, Maggie depended more than ever on mall walking for exercise. Always a loner, she arrived as soon as the mall nearest her office opened for walkers, two full hours before the shops unlocked. She was walking four miles a day now since she had nearly eliminated tennis and swimming because of weekends back and forth with Rick and Beth. Instead of counting her steps, she watched the clock over the information center, allowing herself just under an hour. Now she did much of her private thinking as she walked, hammering out decisions as her feet hit the tiles.

For several mornings she had dredged up everything she could remember from her own childhood religious training, the years in Sunday school and her mother's overly zealous instruction. Memories of revivals in which evangelists at Blakeville Liberty Crossroads Baptist Church had thundered and cajoled, alternately threatening hellfire and promising glory. Of spirited Saturday night singings and sleepy Sunday afternoons after a dinner on the ground the Sunday they decorated the cemetery. Country preachers who could little more than hold up a Bible and declare their confidence in its contents. And of missionaries returning with stories of Black souls saved in Africa but ready to burn the house of a local Black they thought didn't know his place.

Maggie sorted through all the sludge of her own religious upbringing, trying to tell if there was *anything* that she wanted to salvage. Finally she concluded that she could still accept:

*the certainty that God was real and had authority over the world—she was tired of feeling responsible for the success or failure of everything she even remotely touched

*the certainty that some things were unequivocally right or wrong—she was tired of stopping to argue whether in certain extenuating circumstances even the most repugnant behavior might be justified.

*the certainty that something, at least one thing, was true—and why could it not be the Bible?

At the same time she considered her friends: her clients, subordinates at work, the competition, the widows and divorcees that she knew, and decided that she could use a few friends with solid old-fashioned values and old-fashioned faith.

"I never thought I'd come to this," she admitted to herself at last.

Of what John believed she had the only vaguest ideas. She was certain that he had never eaten a piece of pork in his life or shellfish either. For years she had refused to listen to his explanations why. And, of course, she knew Seventh-day Adventists observed Saturday instead of Sunday and far more scrupulously than Baptists usually kept their worship day. She suspected that he still paid tithe to his church in spite of the protests she had made when they were first married and managing on a meager budget. Her husband believed that dead people were really dead until sometime in the future, and that Christ would really come back to the earth to take believers to heaven. Maggie had laughed in his face about that when they were in high school even though Baptists also believed in Christ's return. John said that everything he believed was solidly based on the Bible. But so did the Baptists.

She was not just sure what Rick and Beth believed. Probably something similar to the Baptists. And about Catholics she knew almost nothing except the horror tales she had heard growing up among Protestants. Her college history teachers had delighted in reminding their Bible Belt students that such stories had been created during the Reformation to justify the violent measures taken by politically motivated kings and their henchmen.

Common sense told her that many Catholics sincerely believed they too were following the teachings of the Bible. It also reminded her that the only way to find out what the Bible actually said was for her to read it herself, but after her first and only experience at trying that, she felt incompetent to the task. The last thing she would do, she decided, was to ask someone to study the Bible with her, for such study could be nothing but biased.

Twice on Thursdays at lunch Corrine had brought up her seances. "You just can't imagine, Madge, the pleasure these conversations with Leighton bring me. I've felt absolutely desolate since his passing. You know that. Now I feel that I can go on living—possibly even go on enjoying life."

Maggie hoped she had been civil in the way she changed the subject. Frankly, Corrine's enthusiasm was disgusting. But then, she thought, people mostly accept what they want to believe, and that's why there were so many churches with such divergent doctrines.

Just what is it I hope the Bible will tell me I ought to believe? she asked herself repeatedly. She was almost afraid to explore such an idea.

Did she want it to tell her that the dead did not really die? No, course not. If John died, would she want him looking down from heaven—where he surely would go—observing her fits and pauses, her griefs and frustrations? No.

Did she want it to tell her that God would put up with anything a person decided was right as long as he was sincere? No. Lora's second husband was probably sincere—at least to a certain point.

Did she want it to tell her that she could have her smart clothes and jewelry, the house and all her collectibles— maybe even take than to heaven with her. Possibly. She couldn't imagine herself in a plain white robe just like everyone else was wearing, shouting alleluias. And while a golden crown might be nice, she liked necklaces herself, and earrings. What would heaven be without fine china and paintings and grand pianos?

Maggie was sure the Bible said nothing at all about grand pianos, and she was almost sure that it said nothing about wedding bands although John had been conscience-stricken about buying her one.

Just what did she want to discover in the Bible?

On days when John scheduled surgery, Maggie began returning home after leaving him at the hospital. Feeling guilty because of her secrecy, yet knowing she was doing the very thing he had prayed for, she sat down at the kitchen table with his Bible and a notebook, reading a chapter here, another one there, referring to other texts that John's hand-written notes suggested were related. In the notebook she wrote the ideas that took shape as a result of her reading, trying to make some sense of what she had pieced together before she put the Bible away and went to her office to work out solutions to insoluble financial dilemmas.

As the day of Rick's surgery approached, Maggie tried to bring herself to pray for him and for Pete, even for herself as she felt her nerves straining with anxiety. But whenever she knelt and closed her eyes, she was dismayed by the only prayer she knew—the prayer she had learned as a child.

"Now I lay me down to sleep.

I pray the Lord my soul to keep.

If I should die before I wake,

I pray the Lord my soul to take."

That wasn't at all the petition she meant to make. *Please, God, don't take anybody's soul away now—not mine or John's or Rick's.* Just how did an adult go about praying to God?

Then one morning she discovered the Psalms. Many of them asked for the very things she felt like crying for—forgiveness, courage, physical protection.

"Purge me with hyssop, . . .

wash me, and I shall be whiter than snow" (Ps. 51:7, RSV).

"Out of the depths I cry to thee, . . .
 Lord, hear my voice!" (Ps. 130:1, 2, RSV).
"My soul waiteth for the Lord
 More than they that watch for the morning:
 I say, more than they that watch for the morning"
 (Ps.130:6).

"But I am poor and needy:
 make haste unto me, O God:
 Thou art my help and my deliverer;
 O Lord, make no tarrying" (Ps. 70:5).

Haltingly Maggie began shaping her own prayers.

"Are You there? Are You listening? Listen. Oh, please listen!"

"Does it matter to You that Rick may be dying? Do You care anything at all about us with all You have to think about?"

Words echoed from a revival she had attended as a child—no it was at John's mother's funeral, a plaintive country voice singing.

"Oh, yes, He cares, I know He cares.
 His heart is touched with our grief."

"God, do You care?" she asked.

Maggie wanted to cry out to her husband, "John, does He?" But she was not ready yet to talk to him about what was happening to her soul.

* * * *

The last Saturday before Rick's surgery, John got up at 5:00 a.m. After showering and shaving, he went to his study, taking his Bible with him. But instead of reading, he kept thinking.

Tomorrow Rick and Beth would be here, and Monday Lora would come. He was glad he had today to get ready himself.

Somehow he had expected Maggie to "pitch a fit"—as her mother used to describe her outbursts when she was crossed.

For a month now he had gone to church every Sabbath, and she had been silent—no sarcasm, no ridicule—just an uncommital silence which, as far as he could see, carried no meaning.

"I love you too much, John, to be still while you make a fool of yourself," she had said in white heat when Rick was 6. "If you have to go to church, at least pick one where successful people attend. You don't have to advertise your rural graces."

He had been angry then and hurt, and under the double stress, he had asked, "Do you think, Maggie, that either you or I will ever outgrow our 'rural graces'? What's wrong with 'rural graces' anyway? Have you become so refined you're ashamed of your mother, Maggie?"

"You bet I am," his wife had exploded. "And your mother too. Both of them ignorant, superstitious—both of them frowsy, dowdy lumps of flesh! We were lucky they both died young!"

John knew she meant it. He had always sensed the continuing battle between Maggie and her mother over teased hair, low-cut dresses and short skirts, over movies and rock and roll music. Maggie's mother had made her go with her to the Baptist Church twice every Sunday and to prayer meeting on Wednesday nights. And both Maggie and her mother saw *his* mother as the common enemy. Even in his teens he could recognize that.

"You can't let them make an Advent out of you," Maggie's mother had warned her often, adding before he had closed their front door and was out of hearing, "I can't see what you want Johnny Hamilton for anyway. He'll never amount to a thing, always cottoning to his mama the way he does. You want to live the rest of your life sharing a house with an Advent?"

What he didn't overhear, Maggie repeated later with her own biting additions. She had always made him choose between his mother and her. He and Maggie had gone off to college, and later when they married, they came back only rarely—distancing themselves from any relationships that she feared might lure them back to Blakeville. Her mother had died at 40—of a stroke, a result John guessed of her country cooking and her raging temper. His own mother had been struck down by a reckless 20-year-old driver in front of the general store a year later. It was after her funeral, John remembered, that he gave up going to church—when Maggie had attacked both mothers and the ground had hardly settled on her own mother's grave. Rick had always wondered why John never took him back to his Sabbath school.

I never did tell him anything reasonable, John thought. *Just put him off with feeble excuses.*

How much of that conflict had Rick comprehended? he wondered. Certainly some of it, because it was as if after that the boy saw his world made up of two hemispheres—father and mother. And Rick had established himself firmly in his father's half of his world, always respectful to Maggie, but never close—guarded, protecting himself from her disapproval by not caring too much for her approval. Yet, Rick was his mother's son, for when he made his choice to be a Christian, he broke loose from her control, ignored her ridicule, and built his own life based on his own values. Just as she would have done had she been in his position.

Even with his study door closed, John smelled the muffins Maggie had in the oven. He went to the kitchen in his robe, his bare feet drawing up the coolness of the tile floor as he stood in the doorway watching her swift movements as she sliced an orange and arranged it on a white plate.

"Good morning, John. It's past 7:00. Time you were eating."

* * * *

Just as he entered the church the song leader announced a number in the hymnbook to the 20-some people scattered in the sanctuary. Opening the book to the hymn, John sat and listened to the uncertain voices nearly swallowed by the large room. He did not feel like adding his own thin voice. John had chosen this church because, of the many he had visited during the previous weeks, the congregation seemed the least sophisticated, the most like the Adventist church back in Blakeville. The gray-haired man sitting two rows ahead of him with his 1950 haircut was a mechanic. John had shaken hands with him in the foyer, had noticed the bruised knuckles and the blue nail with another growing beneath it, pushing the damaged one up. Except for three old women and the Sabbath school superintendent, the congregation consisted of men. He knew why, for he could hear the strong female voices in the children's rooms below, three or more women with each group leading toddlers or kindergartners in some of the same songs Rick used to sing. And further back, from under the baptistery, came the sound of a guitar and a young feminine voice and a chorus of juniors lustily singing, "It only takes a spark to get a fire going . . ."

The song service ended and the superintendent welcomed the group to Sabbath school. "Especially our visitor," she said. "We're so glad you're here."

One of the men offered prayer and an older woman read a mission story. The scattered members bunched together for two adult classes, one on either side of the room. John sat down next to a man in his late 20s who was probably a factory worker, nodded to him, and opened his Bible. It was then that he noticed the corner of a slip of yellow paper sticking out of it. He opened to Psalm 130 and stared at the note in Maggie's minuscule block print.

"Though we all of us stumble in the valley of the shadow of death, I will try to fear no evil.

"So help me God."

CHAPTER EIGHT

The teacher of the Sabbath school class asked a member to offer prayer before the lesson study, but John did not so much as close his eyes. Instead he sat staring at the yellow slip of paper, at Maggie's paraphrase of the words from the Shepherd Psalm, too shocked to think or even feel. The prayer ended, and the teacher turned to him.

"Just visiting again," John said in response to the man's sincere greeting. Then he spontaneously added, "I'm an Adventist. I've been a long time away from home. From church, I mean." He glanced at the more than a dozen men and the two elderly women seated around him and thought of his mother in his childhood congregation. "I live here in Atlanta, actually less than ten miles away, but I've been in the 'far country' for a long time."

And then, what he could not tell the chaplain at the hospital he found himself describing to these unpretentious people, recognizing in them the "rural grace" which would accept him warmly, each of them glad to welcome him back though they had not seen him go. To his surprise he told them of his years of silent withdrawal, his involvement in his work and its accompanying lifestyle. He related Maggie's repeated illnesses and now Rick's crisis. Finally, just as he had done scores of times as a child or teen in the Blakeville church's prayer meeting, he ended his testimony with a halting, "Please pray for me."

"Amen!" the people around him responded fervently.

"Why not right now?" the teacher suggested, and without a second thought, the group dropped to their knees. John, a little embarrassed at what he had done, knelt too. As he half listened to their petitions, it became clear to him that Maggie had been reading his Bible recently—more than reading it, absorbing it—and that she had surrendered something in the process. While other voices, filled with tearful emotion, called out to God to help him and his family, he lost sight of the immediate problems in his own silent elation.

"I don't know what this means, Lord," he prayed silently. "I feel too confused to understand how I ought to respond, but thank You."

Matter-of-factly the group arose and moved directly into a discussion of the Sabbath school lesson, one of them catching John's eye occasionally and smiling. But John found himself unable to concentrate on the prophet Ezekiel's anguish. Right now it seemed totally unrelated to his own joy. If God could do this for Maggie, He could—He would surely—do anything necessary to heal Rick.

The superintendent rang a small bell on the pulpit, signaling that the lesson should end. Almost like a tape recorder turned off, the discussion stopped.

"Where's Harriet?" the superintendent asked.

"Downstairs filling in for Lois in Primary," someone said.

"Well, I guess we can sing the closing song without the piano. Number 387."

John took the hymnal from the rack ahead of him, and almost by reflex action, walked to the piano, the book in his hand already open to the song. He sat down and struck the opening chord as the congregation rose to its feet.

* * * *

Maggie had planned to prepare food for several meals along with fresh vegetables and other snacks that would keep John, and the rest of the family, for that matter, as level as possible during the week they would all be together. About the time John left for church, the phone began to ring.

The first call was from Beth.

"We'll be later than we thought, Mom. It looks like Justin might be coming down with a cold, and we can't risk letting him ride in the car with the rest of us. Rick and Pete can't get a cold now."

"So, how . . . ?" Maggie began.

"A friend will bring him down in a separate car, but we still haven't figured out how to manage to keep him isolated once we're there."

"I'll see what I can do," Maggie said.

She hadn't yet finished peeling the carrots when Matt called. "Is John there?"

"No, he's at church " Maggie said, balancing the phone on her shoulder and opening the refrigerator.

"John's at church? On Saturday?"

Maggie found the celery. "Yes, on Saturday."

"I just wondered if there was anything Sally and I can do to make things easier for you this week."

"You could pray a lot," Maggie said. She heard Matt draw his breath in surprise. "Well, you could."

He cleared his throat. "Yes, I guess I could. I'll tell Sally. And call us if there's anything else . . . "

Her secretary called. Yes, the workload had been rear-ranged, and she had reached the construction company in Smyrna and told them to find someone else to handle their case.

"I was just worried about you," the woman added. "What else can I do?"

"Just keep everything moving as smoothly as you can and don't tell anyone where they can reach me. Call only when not to do so would mean disaster. Genuine disaster. Something worse than what I'm going through here."

****

Then it was Lydia and Corrine.

"No, there's nothing you can do. Thanks for calling."

* * * *

Working steadily in spite of the interruptions, Maggie had six ziplock bags filled with six different prepared raw vegetables when Lora phoned at 11:30 a.m.

"Mom, I've decided to come on up this afternoon so I can be there to help you. Can I bring anything?"

"Are you bringing the baby?"

"Yes."

She hung up, wondering what she would do when all of them arrived. "That's all I need," Maggie said in exasperation.

* * * *

John was a half hour later than she had expected. Maggie watched him coming through the carport, his face serene. He opened the door and smiled at her across the kitchen.

"I'm glad you got a blessing out of church," she said, hating the sarcasm that colored her voice. "I could have used a little help here answering the phone." As his smile faded, she felt the frustrations of the morning coalescing into a knot of anger in her middle—not against John, but against the whole human race, including herself.

"I can't stand it," she said, struggling for control. "John, I can't cope."

And instinctively, as she always did when she had no other recourse, she clung to him and cried.

When she finished crying, John still did not know what he had rushed home to find out. The long years of habit prevented him from asking that kind of questions, just as Maggie's silence kept her from giving answers. Instead, they only affirmed their love for each other and nothing more.

They ate lunch without speaking. When the phone rang again, he took the call. It was from one of Maggie's business associates, and he told the person that his wife was not available for even the most urgent problems because of a family medical crisis.

Susan called from the clinic. Dr. Blaine had been unable to see a quite critical case.

"I'm sorry," John said. "Please, Susan. I cannot deal with anything except my private life for at least a week. Check the referral chart."

Until Rick's family came at 4:15 p.m. he had time for only a few hurried exchanges with Maggie, who fled from one task to another, maintaining her balance, he knew, like a child on a bicycle, by moving ever faster.

* * * *

"I'll be in charge of Justin," he announced to Rick and Beth before they got out of their car. "You three go on indoors. We'll come later." The friend who had brought Justin unloaded the baggage and carried it inside while John took his grandson by the hand and started down the block. Lora's car was in the yard when they returned. He hesitated at the door.

"Where will I sleep, Grandpa?" the child asked.

John tousled his hair. "With me. We'll sleep on the porch where Grandma keeps her flowers."

Justin looked up at him without replying, and John was certain that neither of them would sleep much tonight. Both of them would spend the night thinking about tomorrow and the day after that.

* * * *

At 2:00 a.m. when the clock in the upstairs hall chimed, Beth had still not slept. She had listened to Pete's grunts and sighs as he turned in his sleep, no more troubled than a puppy in a warm, safe basket. Although she had decided without hesitation that the child should give bone marrow for Rick, and although she had never once thought the decision was wrong, she worried about tomorrow when Pete would undergo his ordeal. Rick had insisted that he must be with Pete through it all, there to reassure him and hold him whenever possible. But on Tuesday when Rick must himself go to the operating room, who would comfort his son?

77

Pete loved his grandparents, but he had never spent a night separated from his mother and father. He was used to her voice or Rick's calling to him from the adjoining room if he cried out in his sleep or cuddling between them if he hurt. Now he wouldn't even have Justin with him.

Beth had listened to Rick's breathing, which betrayed the fact that although he pretended to sleep, he had spent much of the time since 10:00 p.m. awake. When, past 2:00 a.m., he reached to pat her arm she drew closer to him, rubbing her face against his sleeve.

"Thinking?" he asked.

"A lot."

"I know that it's only natural for families to sacrifice for one another, but I keep seeing Pete's perfect little leg—scarred. It seems like a criminal thing to do. To put a baby through such . . ."

Beth rested her hand over his mouth. "No," she said. "What would he do without you? What is a small scar or even pain, compared to losing you?"

Rick drew her hand to his shoulder and held it there. "We've been through this too many times. I know. But I just keep seeing him under the knife. It's easy to know we're doing the right thing. Feeling right about it is . . ."

He said no more for a long time. Beth lay there beside him, her arm rising and falling with his breath, her heart crying out in fragmentary prayers, and now that the time was so near, unable to force out the dread which her years of trusting God had kept at bay until now.

"Don't cry," Rick said.

But she kept on crying, and she knew that whether or not he shed tears, Rick was crying too. What had become of her faith? Could God honor such a wavering, uncertain thing? Could she even call it faith?

I'm afraid, Beth thought. *Not about the surgery. We've been through worse situations than that. I'm afraid that it won't work, and then . . .*

She had seen people with leukemia, people once robust growing frail, then fragile, then almost nothing until . . .

Beth had seen families starting out with bright plans for the future. Not hopes, but solid plans, money in the bank for a dream house. Career ladders and advancing job descriptions.

And Rick kept reminding her that they had the best insurance policies available. That in any eventuality she and the boys would have whatever they might need. Did those insurance policies themselves indicate that they lacked faith in God's provisions? Rick always said no.

She felt him draw a long breath as if repressing a sob.

"Forgive me, Father in Heaven, but I can't accept all the possibilities yet. Are You trying to tell me that it's my duty to accept something like this as Your will if . . ."

* * * *

Lora awoke near dawn in the room that had been hers all her life. Since she had left home to marry Bob 13 years ago, the room had been redecorated twice and now seemed larger, as if all of her girlhood dreams had been swept from the corners, trashed along with posters showing kittens with pink bows and rock stars and the French horn Mom had always wanted her to play. She missed the way the light beside the back door used to shine through the narrow blinds and the white priscilla curtains. And she missed herself, the girl she had once been, sleeping here, or half awake, still dreaming of romance.

She remembered the summer she had spent her allowance week after week on paperback love stories, lying here curled under a light cover while the air conditioner bathed her face in its coolness, reading until nearly morning of love that faced unbelievable obstacles, never wavering—love always triumphant, always enduring, always coming into its own at last. She had read to the end of each book before turning out her light, then lay dreaming, until sleep overtook her, of herself at the center of such a love affair. And then in the morning, because her mother was already gone to work, lying until nearly noon in bed, her mind again filled with the same wonderful dreams.

What tragic flaw mars my character, she thought, *that keeps me from having what I always dreamed of? Inordinate pride, as the ancient Greeks saw it, or maybe like Nathaniel Hawthorne's recurring theme, a soul that looked for perfection in others and self, and in asking too much, destroyed what might have become almost perfect?*

Or is it fate? Was I predestined before I was born? Was my life star-crossed from the beginning so that no matter how good I was, no matter how hard I tried, I was bound to lose everyone I might love? Or is the whole universe set up by some malignant Someone who takes delight in watching all of us squirm?

What character flaw could anyone find in Rick? Or Beth?

God might have plenty to punish me for, she thought. *But not Rick.*

* * * *

Maggie awoke, startled that she had been asleep, for she had turned off her alarm at 5:00 a.m., 15 minutes before it was set to go off, thinking she would get up directly. Now she would have to streamline the breakfast to make sure that everyone got fed before Pete awakened, since he was to go to the hospital without eating. She told Lora this a half hour later.

"We're alike," Lora said, half asleep, looking at her over a glass of orange juice. "We have to think of every detail and see that it happens on schedule."

Pausing, Maggie stared at her daughter, startled at her tone of voice.

"Sometimes," Lora continued, "I think that has been my greatest liability in my marriages. I can't keep from being a manager. I'm too efficient. I'm too smart. I'm too successful."

Maggie turned back to her omelette, sprinkling the half-cooked surface with snippets of chives and parsley. "A man who is successful himself isn't threatened by a successful wife. Your father hasn't been."

Lora walked toward her. "You're wrong there, Mother. He's felt threatened all his life by both of us. Even worse, he's spent a good share of his life running scared."

A rising wave of nausea swept over Maggie and she stepped back from the oven, staring at the potholder in her hand.

"No," she protested.

"Yes," Lora insisted.

Maggie watched her set the glass down and leave the room as John came in with Justin. *Lora's right*, she thought. *But John has more endurance than the men Lora has married. I'm going to be sick.*

"John," she said, "you're going to have to serve yourself. It's in the oven."

Closing the bathroom door, she gripped the towel bar with both hands. She felt terribly cold, her fingers brittle as ice on the stainless steel, her arms in front of her, thin like a child's arms on a winter morning in Blakeville—she was a child again on the schoolhouse steps, putting on Johnny's coat because she had left hers on the bus. She was riding Johnny's bike because hers had a flat tire, eating his peanut butter sandwich because she hadn't brought her lunch money.

"God, You know, I've been running scared too."

But somehow, that did not seem sufficient excuse for what she knew she had done to John.

CHAPTER NINE

At 10:00 a.m. Pete was back in his private room. John spoke briefly with the doctor in recovery, then went to the room on sixth floor where Rick was now being prepared for the transplant that would take place tomorrow. He sat in the corner by the window, listening to the rustle of nurse's uniforms, the snap of the clipboard over Rick's chart, the instrument cart being wheeled away. The orderly drew the curtain back and nodded to him.

"We're finished, Dr. Hamilton."

John pulled the chair to a position where he could face his son.

"They gave me a sedative, but it hasn't started to work yet," Rick said.

His father leaned forward. "Son, it's been a long time, but I'd like us to pray together before you are too foggy to know I'm praying for you."

Rick's eyes grew soft and his face brightened.

"I never did tell you why we stopped going to church when you were little. I don't plan to tell you now. But I do want you to know, Rick, that I've never stopped praying. I've prayed for you every day since you were born. I'm not sure I can except God to honor my prayers when I haven't had the nerve to confess my faith, even before my own family, but I think He has. I know He will."

"It was Mom, wasn't it?"

"I'm not prepared to talk about all that."

"I knew."

"Your mother has been reading and praying." He told Rick about the slip of paper in his Bible on Sabbath.

"I gave up hoping for that when I still went to kindergarten Sabbath school," Rick said.

* * * *

With Maggie driving, John closed his eyes against the confusion of five lanes of traffic, still frenetic at 8:00 P.M. *Atlanta never shuts down, even on a sweltering June evening,* he thought. *If it isn't a Braves game, it's "Midnight Madness" at some furniture mall. Traffic just keeps spewing from some human artesian spring—hellborn and hellbent.*

No, John thought. *People. God's children. With breaking hearts. Mothers and fathers, sons and daughters, husbands and wives—all rushing to do whatever they can to preserve whatever love and life they have hold of right now. Some of them fools, some of them wise, but all people, all needing God.*

"Lord, what can I do?"

And suddenly, as if he heard a recorded message, he knew the reason for his own breaking heart. Apprehending it all, he struggled to articulate the idea—not in words, only in a settling in and acceptance of the pain. This was his own Mount Moriah, but at this point he was not sure if God would provide a literal lamb.

"Obedience doesn't give me an easy way out, does it, Lord?"

He remembered that the Lamb of God was "obedient unto death—even the death of the cross."

"Maggie," he said, "where are you?"

"The Panthersville Exit."

Her reply startled him, he not realizing until she answered that he had spoken aloud. He considered again, rehearsing the question this time before speaking.

"Maggie, I mean, in the process of salvation, where are you?"

She in turn took her time to consider before she replied. John released the recline lever on his seat and sat erect, studying her expression, watching her lips move as if she were ready to answer.

"Salvation is a very old-fashioned word, John," she said at last.

"Yes, but God's been saving people for thousands of years."

Maggie switched lanes as they approached their exit. "I don't know whether I'll ever be saved. For most of my life I've wanted no part of it. I don't know, John."

"I found a piece of paper in my Bible." Would she be angry that he confronted her? "A piece of yellow paper."

"You never quit praying, did you?" she accused.

"No," he admitted. "For years I was ashamed to pray—ashamed to ask God for anything for myself because I wasn't living the truth, but I kept praying for . . ."

"Truth with a capital T," Maggie interrupted, her face grim.

"I kept praying for my patients and for Rick and Lora—and for you."

"Reading your Sunday school—Sabbath school—lesson was one thing . . ." Maggie stopped for a red light and did not finish until the car ahead of her moved when the traffic signal turned green. "I thought you were just asserting your own stubbornness—making a statement. Praying is another matter. I wasn't prepared for that. When I realized . . ."

John waited. Finally he saw that she was crying.

"How could I ever stop praying for you?" he asked, the lump in his throat growing.

They were pulling into their own driveway before Maggie spoke again.

"You should never have married me," she said, turning off the ignition.

"I know."

He reached to grasp her hand that held the key, a hand as small and hard as a child's. He remembered the voice in the dream. "Hold on to Maggie. I'm holding on to you."

Her eyes glowed in her pale face. "I thought I had made you decide between God and me—thought I had won. But I never had all of you—ever. Did I, John?"

"Sometimes almost. But, Maggie, God didn't create men and women to compete with Him for one another's devotion. He meant . . ."

"I know. I see that now."

He released her hand, walked around the car, and opened her door. They stood for a moment in the twilight, neither of them reaching to touch the other, but closer, John sensed, than they had ever been before.

Through the kitchen window he saw Lora stoop to pick Evyn up. Maggie, spotting her too, started toward the house. John followed.

* * * *

During the following weeks as Rick began his recovery, John talked with him often about faith and living a Christian life, about prayer and healing.

Once after a long discussion Rick tried to define his belief. "It's not an 'either You heal me or I'll . . .' "

"But I keep praying for a miracle anyway," his father interrupted. "You know, son, that any healing is a miracle, regardless of how many doctors God uses to get it started."

But Rick, while he seemed pleased that they were opening up spiritual dialogue between them, resisted any direct discussion about Adventist doctrine.

"I don't know if you realize it, Dad," he said once, "but I've found what I needed in my own church. If you had gone ahead and brought me up an Adventist, I'm sure that I would be as certain as you are that your church has all the Bible truth there is. But you didn't follow through with it, and I found God on my own. Or rather, He found me and led me to a different church. I've been satisfied. I've been saved. I know Jesus and have given Him my whole life."

"I'll respect that commitment," John said, not sure, even as he promised, that he understood his present responsibility to Rick. Although he had failed his son 30 years ago, God had worked out a way for others to give him the Gospel, and even now He had ways . . .

John knew that he had given Lora nothing—nothing in the way of religious training, not even the beginning of it—and no example to follow. And when she had groped toward something more, he had remained silent, as if he gave his blessing to anything at all she thought would make her happy. With each failure, he had offered comfort for the pain, but no solutions to the basic problem.

When she turned to the Catholic Church for spiritual support, he had prayed earnestly but said nothing. And now, the bitterness of her disillusionment blocked off anything he might say.

"I don't want to talk about God, Daddy," she said after Rick's operation. "I wish you'd quit trying to convert me."

The way she said it, even the look on her face, reminded him of Maggie making a similar statement in her teens.

"But I can keep praying, Lord. She might be trying to block You out, but You still have ways."

Six months before John could not have been so certain. Now his certainty increased with every passing day. After their first conversation the evening of Rick's surgery, he and Maggie had cautiously begun to talk about the Bible and prayer, about evidences of God's leading, about miracles and the miracle of forgiveness. The Sabbath after Rick and Beth returned home, Maggie told him she was ready to attend church with him. While his first impulse was to take her to the church he had first attended in May with its glitzie decor and fashionable members, a second impulse warned him not to. If Maggie came to church with him for the first time and thought she would have nothing to give up . . .

No. Better to let her see the plainer Adventists first—the kind of Adventists she remembered from Blakeville. Afterward—well, that was a problem he would have to leave to the Lord. He felt totally unprepared to begin judging his brothers and sisters in the church for whatever adjustments they had made to a changing world—not after his own disastrous adjustments.

CHAPTER NINE

The effusive welcome she received seemed to embarrass Maggie. But, to John, the greatest evidence of the Holy Spirit's work in her heart was the way she accepted everyone. Knowing country people and country ways, Maggie had always distanced herself from both, as if she had to prove to herself that she had never been a part of that way of life. The next Sabbath she allowed a sunburned woman with hands stained from picking blackberries to hug her—had listened politely to the woman's apologies about not remembering her name.

* * * *

Browsing in a book store in August, Lora came upon several self-help books, bought them, and spent her lonely evenings reading. One had a definitely feminist slant, with which she sympathized at times. At other times she found herself angry with the author's biases and strident tone. Two of the books dealt with improving one's self-image by tuning into resources deep in the self in an almost religious way, but to Lora now an approach quite fresh and non-threatening.

One thing for certain, she thought after reading past midnight, stretched on the sofa, *if I'm ever going to get out of this down spell, I'll have to climb out by myself. I'm not a little girl anymore, and no one is ever going to take care of me. Ever.*

She had just finished a chapter dealing with the power hidden beneath the surface of each person's consciousness, mystical power that made it possible for the individual to choose a course of action and to will unlimited success so strongly that success inevitably resulted. The person who had enough faith in self, the book said, could take control not only of her own life, but also of those less decisive who wandered around looking for someone who knew what ought to be done. Lora contemplated the implications of this philosophy in her three marriages.

She had never had any control over her relationship with Bob—except in keeping the apartment immaculate. And even there, her compulsive cleaning had been the result of her own feelings of helplessness. With Carl she had spent all of her time trying to be an ideal wife, submerging her own goals in his. And with Rodnel she had been slave to the romantic dream that she had at last found someone who loved her for herself alone—while he expected fawning attention to reinforce his own anxieties.

I was always giving, she told herself. *Never getting more than token emotional support from anyone in return. No wonder I ended up frustrated and peevish, difficult to live with.*

For a long time she looked at the closed book in her hands.

Well, never again. While she was not ready to adopt the total philosophy she was reading, she could see this much. Living a life devoted to fulfilling the dreams of other people was self-destructive. From now on she would devote herself to creating whatever kind of satisfaction she could manage in her career and in her personal life. If she could do that without hurting others, well and good. But if other people felt put down or threatened, unloved or unappreciated, that was their problem. To be a survivor, she would have to accept the fact that some people were born losers, would never be successful or happy because they were too weak to create their own happiness.

In the kitchen she poured herself a glass of orange juice and walked back to her bedroom, glass in hand. She stood there staring at Evyn's crib, empty now until Friday after-noon.

And whatever things had become clear to her during the evening's reading went totally out of focus. She kicked off her shoes and sat on the edge of her bed and cried.

* * * *

During the weeks since his surgery, Beth had noticed a brief period in which Rick seemed to be improving, but then she realized that instead of actually being stronger, he was only responding to his own desire for the marrow transplant to work. In reality, he was still losing a little every day—not really noticeable on a daily basis, but apparent after a week and obvious after two weeks. At the end of a month, she called his doctor, demanding to know precisely what he had told her husband.

"Why don't you and your husband come in together so we can discuss the current prognosis?" he suggested.

From the tone of his voice Beth could tell that what she had feared was so. She felt the panic rising in her throat like a physical illness as she stood holding the phone long after the doctor had hung up.

* * * *

Rick faced the doctor across the polished desktop. For Beth's sake he wished he could avoid this confrontation a little longer, but she had set up the appointment and insisted that she must go with him. Now after a brief examination of the latest data, his physician was ready to talk.

"It's not working, is it, doctor?" Rick felt relieved that his own voice remained steady.

"At this point," the man began, then hesitated so long that Rick wondered if he would ever go on. "I might as well be honest with both of you. You are doubtless aware from the way you feel, Mr. Hamilton, that your condition shows a steady deterioration that worries me. We still have some other options . . ."

"Which means that there are a few less effective methods of dealing with CML that probably won't work since the bone marrow transplant didn't."

"We won't know, Mr. Hamilton, until we try."

"We'll try every treatment there is," Beth interrupted.

Rick glanced at her and saw immediately that she would hold him to this decision of hers.

"The insurance may not cover everything," he objected.

Beth's jaw was set in an unnatural way. "That doesn't matter. We'll do anything—everything possible, doctor."

Later as they drove home, Rick wondered if he had the fortitude to follow through on Beth's commitment. He thought of the probably long, almost certainly unsuccessful chemotherapy ahead and the hospital bills that were sure to mount to levels which Beth would be unable to pay after his death—not unless she sold the house and . . .

"Don't worry about all that, Rick," Beth said, as if she had been listening to his thoughts. "Just keep on praying."

"Till light breaks through," he finished the line of the song. Now he was not at all sure that God wanted him to live. *Maybe if I keep praying for life and health, I am in direct opposition to God's will*, he thought. As soon as the thought passed through his mind, he shivered.

CHAPTER TEN

Lora fingered the fabric swatches the saleswoman had given her, sensing the textures as she compared their values in the fluorescent light of the showroom. She walked to the front window and flipped the swatches in the natural light.

"The bone white, I think," she said, returning to her client and the saleswoman who had begun talking beside a display of draperies. "I think we want the bone white for the predominating neutral with several related tones . . . maybe in tweed or a played-down abstract figure."

"I have this four-foot porcelain vase," the client said. "You will, of course, have to see it yourself before knowing the colors to set it off to its greatest advantage." The man took the swatches from her, brushing her hand— consciously, she was certain—with his own.

"Of course," Lora said.

She got the message and considered it. *Why not?* Four empty days and nights separated her from Friday at 4:00 p.m. The client had already given enough information— whether accurate or not seemed immaterial now—for her to see that his wife was settled firmly in her career on the West Coast and that their marriage from here on out would be a rather loose attachment, convenient for social and business reasons and for the tax benefits.

Why not? No one will ever take care of me again, Lora reminded herself. *I might as well enjoy whatever pleasure I can get hold of, and maybe I'll eventually learn to be satisfied with a life totally free of illusions. Why not?*

"Why not?" the client asked later after an elaborate dinner in a restaurant.

Lora avoided his face, looking instead at the remnants of veal cutlet and parsley stems.

"I'm not sure," she said. "I find it difficult to explain to myself the idealism that intrudes if any relationship starts to be faintly romantic. You see, my father and mother . . ."

The client clucked condescendingly. "Real prudes . . ."

"Hardly. Still very much in love with each other after being married for nearly 40 years. Any other kind of relationship seems rather shoddy . . ."

The man across the table reached to tilt her chin up. She turned away.

"Does that mean you don't have a right to a little fun? This is a different world with different values and different dreams . . ."

"Whatever you say, it does matter. That's why not."

* * * *

Beth called a cab, not trusting herself to let him drive her home. In the bare apartment she sat down on the featureless couch with the book about creating a new self-image. She read 30 pages, put a letter from the phone company in to mark her place, and prepared for bed, not knowing at this point whether she was a born winner or a born loser. At any rate, she was obviously her parents' daughter. Never could she escape from that reality. The thought was more comforting than it had been on previous occasions.

"At least I can count on that fact to give my life some stability," she muttered as she reached to turn out the light.

* * * *

It occurred to John as he settled in his recliner in the family room and opened his Bible that even though Maggie had attended church with him several times and had talked with him about his faith in God's care, they had never read the Bible together, never prayed together. He considered that thought for a few minutes, then placed his Bible back on the lamp table and got up. Maggie was in the kitchen with something pipping in the pressure cooker while she examined computer spreadsheet printouts at the table. Sitting down opposite her, he watched her fingers moving swiftly over the columns, then stopping suddenly when she located the numbers for which she had been searching.

She circled something, jotted some figures on a note pad, and looked up.

"Will you be working late here?" John asked.

Maggie flashed a look that signaled triumph.

"No, I located the tangle. Between the lawyer and the accountant we can have everything settled in an hour in the morning. I had anticipated spending half the night tracking down the error. John, if I had kept books the way this company does when we were starting out, you would never have had enough money to start a practice."

"I believe it. If you hadn't been a financial genius, I would never have made it through medical school. You've always taken good care of me, Maggie."

She began folding up the spreadsheets, settling all the Z-folds into the file folder before putting the folder into her briefcase.

"I've thought that often enough myself," she said, her tone implying an admission that had been hard for her to come to. She brought a dishcloth and washed the table as if disinfecting it from some moral virus brought in on her business papers. "Lately I've come to realize that most of the choices I've made for us and the kids have been pretty misguided. Business genius, I am willing to admit to. Moral leadership . . . John, you know I used to think I'd never cringe and grovel like a fool before anyone—even God. As if bowing before Him would be degrading. As if acknowledging His authority would mean . . ."

At the sink she still held the dishcloth she had wrung out

minutes before. "What did I think it would mean?"

"I don't know," John answered.

"A return to the mentality of the middle ages? I think I equated faith with the kind of intellectual intimidation that prohibited questions and even thought. Why?"

"I don't know."

"My people weren't even close to the snake-handling, faith-healing wondermen that used to come to the brush arbors in the summer."

"Or the traveling evangelist with his pony cart . . ." John smiled, remembering.

"And goats." Maggie sat down across from him at the table. "John, when we were kids and you talked about being a missionary, I pictured us living like that somewhere in the Kalihari or maybe on the Altiplano. You with your medical supplies in a footlocker inside the cart. A bedroll, a cooking pot, and all those goats trotting along behind, ready to be milked every night when we camped."

"I didn't grow up on that kind of mission stories," he objected. He thought of his childhood heroes crossing the Andes or tracing an Amazon tributary in a plane while in constant contact with headquarters at the hospital. For an instant he saw Maggie at the controls, the craft bucking upward through clouds while he tried to snatch some sleep before the next jungle landing. Laughing, he told Maggie about the fantasy.

She laughed with him but then turned instantly sober. "How many mission planes have you financed?"

He hesitated. "Three."

"I should have known. You've kept a few private accounts of you own all along, haven't you? You've always paid tithe to your church."

Her last comment was not a question. Nor was it, he decided, an accusation, but rather a statement of fact.

"Yes."

"You've always had the courage to do what you believed, John. Even when I was angry about that, I was proud of your courage."

John drew a long breath. "If you only knew how much I compromised, how much I buried under good intentions. The Lord knows that even the mission planes were a kind of payoff, trying to expiate my guilt . . ."

"I'm sorry, John."

"I'm sorry, too, that I didn't have enough faith to risk your anger and . . ."

"Ridicule," Maggie finished for him. "That was my weapon. Always a coward's weapon. Even when I was a little kid I dreaded having the other kids make fun of the dresses my mother sewed, so I made fun of theirs first. Always desperate. As if, if I howled louder and longer, no one would have the energy to turn on me with my own kind of warfare."

"Yes," he said quietly.

"And that's why you could always love me even when I was so terrible?"

"I think so. Intuitively."

Maggie had been staring at her hands, but now she looked up, her eyes meeting his and holding them. "How does a person make something like that right?"

John reached across the table. "Just ask. Just be willing to ask God to forgive."

A bleak smile touched her lips. "I never liked to ask for anything. You know that."

"But asking is part of acknowledging that God can do what we can't," he insisted. "That He wants to."

When Maggie began to pray, he sensed that she had been rehearsing her prayer for some time, that she had prepared a mental list of sins for which she felt conviction, and that she confessed to him even as she did to God. When she finished at last, he added his own prayer for forgiveness, feeling with each admission part of the heaviness under which he was accustomed to live roll away.

* * * *

Walking in the mall the next day, Maggie felt the muscles in her back flexing with her stride in a new and comfortable way, almost as if some of her inner fabric had become more elastic. The pain that usually accompanied any kind of exercise was little more than a tenderness that made her aware of her muscles as she took the second flight of stairs. She walked faster on the third level, past the quilt displays from the various Georgia counties. Log Cabin, Lone Star of Texas, Double Wedding Ring, and newer patterns, but even most of them variations of traditional patterns her grandmother had pieced together 50 years ago.

Same old basic patterns, Maggie thought.

In her memory she could visualize the Blakeville women around the quilting frame set on the backs of kitchen chairs in the living room—taking up the whole floor. She could see their intense concentration, each of them careful that her stitches were smaller and more even than her neighbors so that she could comment on the fact later at home.

"Maybelle's eyesight's failin'," Granny would tell Mama as they washed supper dishes. "You'll have to take out some of her work. Peggy quilts just like her ma did. Knots and tails in every seam."

Maggie thought of the four or five quilts in a cedar chest at home, all wedding gifts from neighbors or relatives. She had never spread one on a bed, for it was as if she did display their traditional patterns, she would be acknowledging the authority of her country heritage and John's over both their present and their future.

The Dove in a Window, she thought, would be just the right color for her bedroom with the muted colors she had there now. She was glad, at least, that she had never packed the quilts in moth balls. The smell of mothballs . . .

* * * *

"Maggie tried to explain to me something about not playing golf on Saturday afternoon," Matt told John over the phone. "It was all a bit confusing."

"I suppose so," John replied.

"She said something about going to church."

John wondered how to begin telling friends who had

known him for years that at last he was coming out of spiritual hiding.

"I'm stripping off my camouflage," he told Matt. "I've been trying to keep anyone from knowing for so long, that the game has grown old. I'm a Seventh-day Adventist, always have been, and always will be. Not a very good one, but still a Seventh-day Adventist."

"Had me fooled!"

"When I had my back up against the wall, I realized it was no good trying to play games with God. Either I was or I was not a Christian. I decided I was."

"That's all right with me," Matt commented. "But how about golf Saturday afternoon? Say 5:30 when it starts to cool off a little?"

John glanced at the calendar on the opposite wall. "There are a lot of things you won't grasp right off. Like the fact that to a Seventh-day Adventist the whole day is sacred, not just the 11:00 church time. I know that sounds strange after 20 years of Saturday afternoons on the golf course, but . . ."

"Well, what about Sunday evening then?"

* * * *

Sunday morning John thought they might have to call the golf date off because of overcast skies that seemed to be lowering in, but then toward mid-afternoon the clouds lifted. When he and Maggie got out of the car at the club, he was surprised by the pleasant breeze from the southeast. They were halfway around the course when he realized the clouds had dropped again and that the grass had taken on an unnatural greenness.

"We'll have a storm directly," Matt agreed when John commented on it.

But they continued to play until the rising wind interfered with their shots.

"Come on over to the house for the evening," Maggie invited the couple. "I'm not done enjoying the two of you yet."

The women decided they wanted to ride together, so

John got into Matt's car with him.

"I've been wanting to ask you about Rick," Matt said after they left the club's long driveway and were headed toward the freeway. "I've spent the whole time so far talking about trivia while the true value of friends is to provide ears to hear about life's real woes."

"We haven't heard anything new for a couple of weeks," John said. "Naturally we're hoping that means that everything is looking good."

Matt glanced over his shoulder to check traffic before pulling off the entrance ramp. "You know," he said, "I was a bit caught off guard at the time of the surgery when Maggie threw me that little suggestion about praying for all of you. To be honest, I've always believed a person ought to pray about serious matters, but it seemed somewhat out of character for Maggie. You know what I mean?"

"Maggie has surprised me lately—and we're talking about major shocks." John hesitated. "Funny how we've been married for nearly 40 years, and now I discover how little I really knew about her."

"Or she's been changing a little at a time and you didn't notice," Matt suggested. "Through the years both Sally and I have changed a great deal. You know, the past two years with all the . . ." He paused. John glanced at him, noticing the way his jaw had set. "When Leighton died . . ." Matt went on. "It makes a person realize that not even you and I are immortal. I used to feel we were—that by benefit of some intellectual inoculation we were immune to the usual devastations that come after middle age. What I mean is that many of the things I rejected as unimportant 20 years ago have come to seem rather important lately."

"Like?" John watched the beginnings of a smile play around Matt's mouth.

"Sally. Surprising how much I had taken for granted that I could always count on her to manage the best she could whether I had time to appreciate her or not. I guess what I mean is that I figured my marriage was just a background for all the other things in my life, providing an appropriate setting for my career, so to speak."

"Without Maggie I wouldn't have a career," John said.

Matt nodded. "I could see you felt that way as long as I've known the two of you. Sometimes I thought you were a fool to be that dependent on a woman, and other times I thought anyone who didn't recognize Maggie's value as a partner would be an absolute fool. But Sally's really a background person, if you know what I mean. I didn't realize until about a year ago that without all she does to give me an emotional foundation, I would be in as bad shape as you would be without Maggie's financial savvy. The idea was humbling."

John laughed.

"Don't laugh," Matt said, almost sharply. "At Leighton's funeral I started thinking about what some strange clergyman, called in for the occasion and never having seen me alive, would intone over my dead body in a few years. And I wondered how much comfort what he said would be to Sally. After all, she's always been something of a Christian of sorts. Subscribing to *Guideposts* and buying religious Christmas cards. That kind of thing. Never saying much, but thinking quite a bit. I suppose she'd go to church if I'd go with her."

Having taken the expressway exit, Matt was signaling at the first traffic light. John expected him to say more, but he was silent. Large raindrops began to hit the windshield, then a few bits of hail.

Matt looked at him. "Tornado?" He flicked on the radio, tried a few stations, all of them popping with static, then turned it off again.

"When I first guessed I might have diabetes," John said, "I thought it was the beginning of the end for me. It's surprising how insignificant an illness like that can become in the face of possibly losing a son."

"I suppose so."

"And to tell the truth, the relief of changing my lifestyle to match my convictions has been far more . . . ."

John stopped mid-thought as a branch torn from a tree ahead crashed into the street, then rolled like a giant tumbleweed until it lodged against the tree trunks on the other side of the street.

He knew that Maggie and Sally were already at the house, for Maggie did not hesitate in traffic the way Matt had. John said no more until they pulled into the drive. Maggie, standing at the window, went quickly to open the garage door.

"Drive on in," he told Matt. "No telling what kind of blowing debris might damage your car out here."

CHAPTER ELEVEN

The highway was glutted with traffic—*people like themselves*, Maggie thought, *cutting short a pleasant Sunday evening, hoping to get home before the storm hit.*

"I've never thought of you as a particularly religious person," Sally commented.

Maggie glanced swiftly at her then back at the car ahead of her, signaling now, but not moving into the exit lane. "You're right about that, Sally. I've spent quite a bit of energy downing religion of any kind for as long as I can remember. Now I'm rather surprised at myself."

"Well, then, are you a Seventh-day Adventist too?"

"I . . ." Maggie realized that she had no idea just what she was. "I don't know," she admitted.

Sally laughed. "That's the first time I've ever heard you say, 'I don't know.' "

Maggie drew in her breath. "It's the truth. I've spent most of my life making assertions . . . as if by asserting something, I proved it was so. I'm beginning to see that I don't have that kind of authority. I can't make things I don't like go away just because I yell." She felt a knot let go in her diaphragm as she acknowledged the fact to her friend. "When I was a kid, I thought whoever yelled the loudest—or at least whoever was still yelling when the other kids went home to supper—was the winner. But that isn't so, is it?" She glanced again at her friend.

"No," Sally said.

"As far as being a Seventh-day Adventist is concerned," Maggie backtracked, "I'm hardly one. John grew up in that church and has always believed that way. I've lived with him all these years and never allowed him to tell me anything. I've been going to church with him lately because we both need God. But I don't know enough about his church to have any idea whether I agree with them or not." She thought for a moment about what she had just said. "I believe in God, and I am sure John knows God in a way I want to know Him."

Even trying to sort out her feelings left her exasperated.

"I've never been comfortable about a church connection," Sally said. "I guess, if Matt . . . No, even if Matt offered to go with me, I probably wouldn't be a churchgoer. But I do believe in miracles, and I do pray. I prayed for you when you said we should. I felt . . . I felt God was really near to me then, and I felt certain that He was doing something for Rick because I was praying for him."

"I appreciate that, Sally." Maggie gripped the steering wheel tighter as the wind buffeted the car like some monster intent on destroying them.

"Look!" Sally pointed toward the K-mart parking lot ahead. A dozen or more shopping carts, jammed together, rushed like an express train before the wind. "Somebody's car is going to get it."

Maggie watched a baby stroller take off from the Good-will deposit box at the corner, and a box of toys that had been sitting beside it overturned—balls, toy trucks, and clothing flying into the street. A ball bounced off her hood, and a pink toddler-sized sleeper clung momentarily to her radio antenna before the wind tore it loose.

Five minutes later, pulling into her own yard, she pressed the remote control that raised the garage door. Once inside, she felt weak.

"I hope the fellas don't get hit by anything," Sally said.

They stationed themselves beside the kitchen window where they would see Matt's car approaching.

Maggie made sandwiches, and later the four of them sat comfortably in the living room, half listening to the evening news and carrying on a fragmented conversation.

"Maggie, seeing your brass collection is almost like visiting a fine museum display," Matt said, getting up for a closer look at the case nearest him.

John watched the pleasure brighten his wife's face as she opened the glass door and handed a Far Eastern bowl to Sally. He saw her turn to Matt, her eyes unshadowed by worry for once.

"Do you remember the Knoxville World's Fair?" Maggie asked him. "I visited the displays from Cambodia six or seven times . . . Far more interesting than the gold from Peru or even the porcelains from China."

"I was fascinated by the Chinese terra cotta," Sally said.

"But the brass," Maggie went on, "was something wonderful. I had been picking up a piece now and then before that, like these English sugar casters and matching creamer, but I really began collecting after the Fair."

John remembered her passionate winter remodeling the house to accommodate her collections, their arguments about how much space they really needed, and finally her victory—adding this large room to the house they had lived in since the children were small. There at the end of the room hung the last painting he had purchased—purchased at Maggie's insistence, as if she would force him to collect things too. And in the wide hallway leading to the dining room his own paintings hung, a record of the hours he had spent struggling with inner pressures and ideas that he could articulate in no other way.

At least for me, he thought.

"Sometimes I think of all this brass as a personal collection of household gods," Maggie was telling Sally. "You know, as if possessing beautiful things would in some way transfer . . ."

The phone rang. Maggie closed the cabinet door and

went to answer it. John pondered what she might have meant to say. Suddenly he heard an unnatural gurgling sound in her throat as she tried to speak, and he rushed to her in the hallway.

"Rick died an hour ago," she said.

* * * *

It took them two hours to reach Cleveland, Tennessee. Cars lined the street and filled the driveway in front of their son's house.

We're ten miles from Blakeville, John thought as he held Maggie's hand, waiting for someone to come to the door. *Ten or eleven miles from Blakeville. Almost home.*

Beth's father came to the door. John shook his hand and led Maggie into the family room where Beth sat, surrounded by friends and relatives. The way widows used to do, he thought, in the Blakeville of his childhood. Already the room had taken on that atmosphere, that hush of women intent on setting things to rights in the bedrooms and kitchen, of coffee smells and food already on the table, as if feeding the bodies of the grief-stricken family was the best way to help them survive.

In his dreams, for 30, years he had witnessed scenes like this whenever he had lost a patient. He had always tried to push the images farther away, out of sight, so that he could muster his skills and possibly save the next person.

But this was Rick's house filled with mourners. This was Rick's widow. Somewhere in all this ritualized hush Justin and Pete huddled—his son's orphans. *I can't even pray*, he thought. *Oh, God, I can't even pray. Forgive me. I can't pray!*

Maggie's hand was small and cold.

"Lora?" Maggie asked no one in particular.

"She said she'd come in the morning," Beth's mother answered.

They must submit, John realized, to being comforted by strangers whose intentions were kind if sometimes clumsy. He braced himself for the ordeal and held his wife's hand even tighter.

CHAPTER ELEVEN

In low murmurs around the room he heard the details of what Beth had told Maggie on the phone. A minor infection, suddenly fullblown in a matter of hours, and death before even Rick's doctor sensed a critical situation. Hardly a fever the night before. A mild fever at breakfast time. Hesitating to phone the doctor on a Sunday, the man's only day to relax. Calling the doctor finally when the fever rose so swiftly. Death swift and nearly painless, when Rick had steeled himself for a long and painful goodbye.

"Providential," a voice murmured.

John felt the heads across the room nodding in agreement.

Providential, he had thought hundreds of times when a patient he had expected to linger had died suddenly. Yet, was death . . . could it ever be . . . providential? What on earth could it possibly provide?

". . . a way of escape, that ye may be able to bear it." Maybe.

"Sit down," said a woman at his elbow as she took hold of Maggie's other hand, drawing them toward Beth's sofa with the cat-embroidered pillows that Justin loved to play with. Two of the women who had been sitting there rose and moved away. He sat down beside his daughter-in-law and looked at her, recognizing in her eyes the numbness he felt himself, the same need to be alone while the reality of death took shape, but at the same time needing all these people here to affirm their support.

An hour later he sat on the edge of Justin's bed, holding the boy's small body against his chest.

"Daddy's gone to heaven," Justin said. "He said he was going." The child twisted his head, and John felt the wetness of his tears on his neck. "He said he wanted to be with Jesus, but why didn't he want to be with Pete and me?"

"He didn't want to leave you," John whispered, rubbing Justin's back, swallowing hard.

What could he say? That God had snatched Rick away from his family? That this was for the best after all?

You can't tell that to a 4-year-old . . . It's not rational even to an adult.

Much later, lying beside Maggie in the bed they always occupied when visiting here, John wondered if there was anything rational he could tell himself about Rick's death. *No, nothing at all,* he thought. *Just like sin, death makes no sense at all.*

Beside him Maggie began to cry. Pulling a pillow closer and making a place for her to curl against him, he held her for a long time before he tried to speak.

"Even in a year, we wouldn't have been prepared," he said finally. Maggie sighed, and her breath was cool against the side of his face.

"I can't understand what's happening, John. You've been praying. I've found God when I wasn't looking for Him . . . while I was running away from Him."

John stretched in the dark for a tissue from the table beside the bed. Maggie blew her nose, and he handed her a second tissue. He felt awkward trying to express the path his thoughts were taking.

"For a while," he said, "I almost bargained with God. If He would heal Rick, then . . ."

"No," Maggie said. "You can't manipulate God that way."

"I know."

"You can't work Him into a corner and deal with Him. I knew right away, as soon as I heard Him speaking to me at all, that I couldn't dictate the terms the way I would with a bankrupt client. I was the one bankrupt, not . . ."

"I know," John repeated. "It was almost as if I expected a miracle to heal Rick, I actually blamed God for making him sick in the first place . . . as if He struck Rick with leukemia in order to bring us to our senses. I can't believe that He did, even though . . ." He fell silent, then said, "But I never doubted he could perform a miracle. So now I keep wondering why He didn't."

"He doesn't have to explain anything to us," Maggie said. "We can't demand for Him to."

CHAPTER ELEVEN

"But . . ."

She drew back ever so slightly.

" 'My soul waiteth for the Lord,' " she quoted. " 'More than watchmen for the morning.' "

That was the place in Psalms, John remembered, where he had found her slip of yellow paper—the one that had revealed to him that she had been reading his Bible.

"I saw He couldn't do anything for us unless we gave in and allowed Him total control," she continued. "I haven't the foggiest idea where He's taking us, but I've given up, John. I'm not arguing with Him any more."

He was about to speak when Maggie went on.

"When I realized how much I had done to hurt you and that you still loved me after all the times—I could see that surely God would do the same."

The following morning he discovered that the details people usually have to attend to after a member of the family dies had, indeed, been arrived at through thousands of years because they helped a person to stumble through a time when one could not face sitting and thinking.

Driving to Blakeville, he personally instructed the man with the backhoe where to dig the grave beside his parents, beside his grandparents, aunts, and uncles. While the man drove stakes to mark the location, John read the names of people he had loved. Still loved but in a different way, he realized as he wandered from grave to grave, thinking of eternity but caught in the present with its July heat and streams of sweat trickling down his scalp and on down the back of his neck, soaking his shirt between his shoulder blades.

When he, out of habit, thought about his father, buried here, as gone, forever gone, he forced himself to reconsider the possibility that even in Dad's case there might be a possibility of meeting him in heaven. *I don't know all that he believed or how he responded to God*, John reminded himself. *Look how I've been wrong all this time about Maggie—or at least for some time I've been wrong.*

Dad—bitter. Dad—vindictive. Insisting that any kind of

religion was meant to keep people from getting out from under the thumbs of other people—meant as a means of keeping his only son from expressing his manhood, his independence from women and the church. John knew that his father and Maggie had formed a league long before his mother had died, intent upon prying him away from his mother and from God. As he stood there now, staring at the headstone on which his parents' names were joined, he wondered if God had been able to salvage his father. *Probably not. But . . .*

The backhoe operator started his machine, and John stepped over the low marker at the foot of the grave. "MOTHER." Amid matted grass clippings from mowing after mowing and weathered sweetgum balls, the narrow marble slab testified to the persistence of his mother's commitment to what she believed and to her prayers for him that had kept working for him long after he had buried her beside the church she loved.

The backhoe's scoop gouged into the red soil between the stakes, leaving space beside the settled graves of his parents.

Space for Maggie and me, John thought, adding out of habit, *If time lasts*. His mother had died at 42, his father at 57.

Time doesn't have to last at all, he mused as the scoop took a second bite into the earth. *I'm mortal with the same brand of mortality—disease or accident. Rick didn't have to grow old to die.*

CHAPTER TWELVE

All those hypocritical songs," Lora said. "Mom! It's a cheap excuse people make when God seems to turn a deaf ear. How do we know He hears anything we say? Or even that He's there in heaven where He claims to be? Maybe He's dead. Or maybe He never was. Maybe we each invent Him for ourselves to be what we hope He'll be for us."

Maggie sat looking out of the limousine window where John still stood with Beth and her parents, his arm around Beth's shoulders, his own heaving with sobs.

"My mother invented her own God," Maggie said, evenly spacing the syllables to control her feelings. "He was like her, always looking for some fault to condemn, some excuse for not keeping a promise. I suppose a lot of people do that. But because they do . . . that doesn't erase the reality of a God who answers to none of us. God is What He is because . . . because He wants to be . . . our Saviour . . . whether we believe it or not."

"Then why didn't He save Rick?"

"He did."

"Here. Now."

Straightening her back, Maggie forced herself to look away from John and Beth. "I don't know. Do we have to know the reason for everything?"

"Can religion give us anything if it can't give us answers?"

"If it can give forgiveness, that kind of saving seems enough."

"How do you know you need forgiveness? Who told you you've sinned?"

"You did. Often enough."

Maggie saw Lora's hand flash out, almost touching her skirt, but she pushed it away. Suddenly she opened the door and burst out of the limousine only to stop and turn to Lora. "I didn't need to be told! I always knew it!"

She let go the tears she had been holding back and ran to John. She felt Beth's arms around her even before he touched her, and then his arms too around them both. For a moment she remembered that she had scoffed at such grief as maudlin, shoddy like the plastic flowers blanketing country cemeteries after an annual decoration Sunday. Whatever she used to think had nothing to do with how she felt now, for she knew she had never really loved Rick as a mother ought to love her son, and he had never really loved her as a son ought to love his mother. Now . . .

* * * *

"He wouldn't give in," Maggie explained to Beth after John had gone to bed with Justin and Pete. "I had it in my head that I had to be in control . . . make him into the kind of person I was. He was always respectful, even in his teens. But I never controlled him."

Beth sat across the kitchen table from her, a coffee cup between her hands. "Rick was like you," she said. "At first. He wanted to control everything. Always very considerate of my feelings, but needing to be in control. After a while he came to understand that only God has the right to do that. By the time we had the boys . . ."

Maggie swallowed. "He was like John—the way he managed the boys."

"He admired his father very much. Loved him very much."

"I know. I wanted to tell him. I didn't know how to do it. Lately . . ."

"We've been praying for you for a long time," Beth said.

* * * *

Lora stared at the rain washing in waves down her windshield, the parking lot floodlight catching the waves as if they were glowing on a shore still luminous in its wetness long after twilight. Momentarily she turned the key on to light the time on the instrument panel: 11:05 p.m. She ought to be on her way. Already she had been here more than an hour, unable to nap as she had hoped she might before starting for Savannah.

Why did it have to rain again? There had been nothing but rain and sodden heat since Rick had died. Except for a couple of hours this afternoon during the graveside service, with everyone standing around, their feet damp, staring at the sodden cemetery grass and the slick edges of red clay oozing from under the fake grass carpeting the mound behind the burgundy and gray tent and the somber chairs around the hole.

Lora reached to start the car but hesitated again, unable to leave Blakeville. This was not the Adventist churchyard, but rectangular pools of water reminded her of how the earth sagged in parallel rows behind gravestones, every pool reflecting some part of the light from the church's parking lot. Across the highway, down the road, in the Adventist cemetery, bedraggled carnation and gladiolas sprays blanketed the red clay pooling down around the edges of Rick's casket. Chunks of chert, like bone fragments, were washed white under the pounding rain.

I should have stayed, Lora thought. "No," she said aloud. *We can't stand each other's comforting. It's too much.*

She felt the tightness of words shaping in her mouth again. "God? What kind of game is this?"

God's not there. I'm as much a fool as anybody else, imagining Him when I can't function rationally on my own.

Leaning her head against the steering wheel, she shut her

eyes, her mind careening through a desperate prayer. "God, if it weren't for Evyn, I'd just as soon be there beside Rick. So much of me has died. And more of me just keeps dying. Why can't I just be totally dead?"

It was midnight, then ten minutes past, when she turned on the radio and caught the last of the hourly news. More rain, they promised. Seventy percent chance tonight and tomorrow. Clearing on the weekend. After that information, return to easy-listening, everything sentimental and sorrowful, but at least not pretending to be happy.

Lora wondered if it was fair to say that Rick and Beth had pretended to be happy. Even now, Beth had memories. She had smiled once during the service, as if with some secret happiness that survived and would reemerge after a while to renew her and give her reason to start again. Mom and Dad? It was unforgivable how they could comfort each other at a time like this. Mom would always have Dad to run to.

I'm jealous, Lora admitted to herself. *Whatever else they're wrong about, Mom and Dad still have each other, and I'm a spoiled kid pitching a fit because I want someone too.*

She noticed the rainwater pulsing in waves out of the grass, over the asphalt curb beside the car. It ran in a stream two feet wide ahead of the car, along the edge of the grass to the right another hundred feet, and finally swirled through a grate into a storm sewer. Her eyes followed the stream back to the left side of her car, mesmerized by the rhythm of the water. The stream slowed as if clotted by something, debris or grass clippings, then broke loose, tugging an angleworm still caught in the grass until it floated out of sight behind her left front tire.

That's me, she thought.

The angleworm reappeared beyond her right fender, roiling in the water, dead or dying.

That's definitely me, she thought again until she noticed other worms following. The sweet-sad music on the radio made her sick. Turning it off, she started the engine. She backed up, then headed out of the parking lot and drove through Blakeville, past the Adventist churchyard where

Rick was buried, past the drugstore at the corner where they turned to go to Dad's childhood home, past the Baptist churchyard where all Mom's people lay buried, finally onto the freeway on her way to Savannah.

The windshield wipers kept the glass clear. The white lines along the edge of the pavement defined safe space. The reflectors marked her own lane, and she kept in it, driving faster and faster as if Blakeville might catch her and hold her there.

I'll never go back to that mentality, she promised herself an hour later when she felt almost out of its magnetic reach. It was 4:00 a.m. when she unlocked her apartment door. Stepping numbly from her shoes, she lay down on her bed and rolled over once, wrapping the comforter around her body.

She awoke at noon, her clothing pulling uncomfortably under her arms, her hair sweaty. Getting up, she reset the thermostat and listened for the air conditioner to kick on.

* * * *

Corrine, always careful to observe social conventions, had called beforehand. "Is it all right if I come over just to be with you?"

Maggie had cast about mentally for some reason she should wait for a few days, but had realized that if one of Corrine's children had died, she would have gone to her uninvited, even unwelcome.

Her first impulse was to vacuum the hallway, but after plugging the vacuum in, she changed her mind and turned the oven on. She would make muffins.

I'm not myself, she thought as she put the vacuum back in the closet. *I'm never indecisive.* She glanced at the clock. Twenty minutes if Corrine came straight over. Setting out the ingredients, she greased the muffin pan.

As she reached for the mixing bowl, Maggie remembered squirming in Mama's sitting room the morning of Granny's funeral while all the neighbors stood like cattle in a loading chute, sweating and crowding around the coffin with about the same amount of intelligence. She remembered the feel of the cushion Granny had crazy-quilted of yellow and red velvet—of holding it in her lap. As she had fingered the black feather stitching that covered Granny's smooth seams, she had wondered if after all there might not be something to be said for believing the preacher. And for a moment she had allowed her imagination to create a presence for Granny, a gossamer foggy something on its way to God yet reluctant to leave her, almost preferring her company to God's. But even in imagination she could not impose upon this spirit angelic sweetness, but only a faithful reproduction of Granny's bent and sinewy form, and instead of seraphic music, Granny's venomous whisper.

Maggie remembered that even then, when she was only 11, the preacher's idea had not worked. She could not piece together a heaven like that and make sense of it. Unless she imagined God was like Granny.

As she measured flour and baking powder, the day in the restaurant when Corrine had told her about the seances flashed into her mind. During the months since then a lot of things had become clear. But that issue had not. Maggie knew now that she had been evading it as if any kind of certainty about death was a dangerous thing. She had been like the people who put off making a will as if the document somehow made death legal. Not even Rick's leukemia had made her willing to face the subject.

As she spooned the batter into the baking pan, she thought how Beth had taken so much for granted about what they had believed in common. *Probably,* Maggie thought, *because she knew I came out of Blakeville's Liberty Baptist Church and had heard all that preaching on the topic.*

Yesterday John had wanted to talk about death in general—had read passages to her and had left lists of texts for her to look up.

"Not yet," she had told him.

Maggie was bent over the open oven, checking the muffins, when she heard Corrine's car in the driveway and went to open the door. With a shudder she realized that her friend couldn't be put off as easily as Beth or John.

Later, Maggie spread margarine on a warm muffin while watching Corrine, who sat across the table, nibble on hers. Corrine glanced at the margarine, then decided, Maggie knew, against the calories.

"I know you're devastated," Corrine began. "I would be. Rick was so young—had so much of life ahead of him."

Maggie bristled. She had heard those words a hundred times since Sunday.

"No," she said. "If it had been John, not Rick . . . That would have been worse."

Corrine nodded and picked up a napkin. "For you. But in general . . ."

"Death never happens in general."

Changing her mind, Corrine spread margarine on the second half of her muffin.

"Maggie, you're positively skeletal. You look terrible."

"Give me a few days." She went to the refrigerator for something and forgot what. Instead of returning to the table, she escaped to the utility room and closed the door behind her. A moment later Corrine followed.

"I'm sorry," Corrine said. "I wish you'd let me talk about the things I've learned about death and separation. It would be such a comfort to you. You need it."

"No, I don't."

"You'd feel so much better. I do."

"How I feel about it won't change the facts." She stared at the detergent box still on the washer. "I won't feel satisfied grabbing for shadows."

"Facts?" Corrine scoffed. "All my life I've been bludgeoned by facts. Don't you see that what you and I experience has some validity, some bearing?"

Maggie set the detergent inside the cabinet.

"I've been wrong about almost everything I felt was certain," she said. "I've come to see that I can't believe my feelings. I'm not sure you ought to believe yours."

And even though she had determined not to break down under Corrine's sentimentalism, Maggie plunged into a recital of her spiritual journey—first away from God, turning her back on Him mostly because He seemed too much like Blakeville . . . looking for intellectual freedom and a materially rewarding life—and then rushing back to Him after all these years away. Maggie stopped her headlong account finally because she needed to blow her nose.

"But traditional religion . . ." Corrine began.

Shaking her head, Maggie reached for a roll of toilet paper on the shelf above the washer. She blew her nose and unrolled a double length of tissue into her left hand.

"I've been reading," Corrine resumed.

"So have I," Maggie interrupted. "The Bible. And I've discovered the difference between feeling and knowing."

"But traditional religion," Corrine insisted, "overlooks the instinctive world that exists as a primary reservoir in our subconscious. It overlooks the power each of us has as a human birthright to tap into those wellsprings of power and awareness and find our own divinity."

Corrine was quoting her own "scriptures," Maggie realized.

"Personally," she said, "I feel safer believing in God and trusting Him to take care of me than to be god myself and have to take care of myself and everybody else. I've been trying that long enough to know I don't have the credentials."

Maggie stared intently at the tissue wrapped around her hand and allowed herself to cry while Corrine hovered her back to the kitchen table.

For an hour she let Corrine mother her—to clean up after their lunch, to run a load of laundry, to water the plants—*comforting small amenities*, Maggie thought as she sat at the table nursing a coffee cup and growing calmer.

"You don't need to stay," Maggie said. "I'll be all right."

"I'm not leaving. I can't leave you here alone."

"I wish you would."

* * * *

After Corrine left, Maggie went to the sunroom with John's Bible.

"Well, Solomon," she said, opening to Ecclesiastes, "I'm giving in here too." It took her a while to find the passage she remembered. "A living dog is better than a dead lion."

Not much comfort there. But the next verse declared, "For the living know that they shall die: but the dead know not anything, neither have they any more a reward; for the memory of them is forgotten. Also their love, and their hatred, and their envy, is now perished; neither have they any more portion for ever in anything that is done under the sun."

Just the way John said it was. Stunning. Alarming.

No, Maggie decided, rather it was comforting when she stopped to think of the helplessness Rick would feel if he were really in heaven, unable to do anything about the inevitable tragedies that awaited Beth and Justin and Pete.

The next verse was even more surprising. After all those hard facts, Solomon advised, "Go thy way, eat thy bread with joy, and drink thy wine with a merry heart; for God now accepteth thy works. Let thy garments be always white, and let thy head lack no ointment."

Maggie read the chapter to the end and then started at the beginning and went through it again.

Live joyfully.

Work diligently.

You don't know how long you'll have all this.

John had carefully written other texts in the margins, but right now she was satisfied with this much information. John believed in a resurrection. Doubtless in good time she would find that documented in the Bible too. She closed her eyes, half praying, and fell asleep.

Chapter Thirteen

When John left the operating room, he noticed that his hands trembled and realized that his blood sugar was low. Instead of the three hours he had expected, the procedure had taken more than five. Yet, although he felt physically exhausted, he was elated about this patient's prognosis. Two weeks ago when they discussed her situation, he had been able to offer her little hope.

"Outcomes like this are what give me faith in what I'm doing," he told his colleague as they walked toward the cafeteria.

The other doctor opened the door and motioned him to go ahead. "Yes, it does feel good to . . . to know that the whole thing was a success . . . that we didn't just prolong the situation."

John remembered Maggie's assertion several weeks earlier that he saved people from cancer so they could die of heart disease, while she rescued them from their creditors so the IRS could get them. He picked up a tray and moved with the line.

When they sat down at a table, John downed a half glass of juice the way he used to gulp a root beer when he was a kid. After looking at the glass a moment, he drank the other half. *God saves*, he thought. *Men help.* "It's too soon to promise anything," he told the other physician. "But at times like this I wish I had the authority to make promises—to know I could promise happiness and long life."

Repeatedly the thought echoed through his mind as he saw patients at the clinic that afternoon. When he and Maggie had dinner with Matt and Sally that evening, he wanted to bring up the subject of certainties, but instead he and Matt talked about golf while Maggie and Sally discussed investments.

After Maggie had fallen asleep hours later, John lay thinking.

Rick's death had settled things that might have taken years to resolve in the normal evolution of human emotion. He had been at first shocked at the relief he had felt almost immediately, as if once what he had long dreaded finally happened, it could never happen again. And during the past few weeks his relationship with Maggie had become almost what he had dreamed in romantic adolescence that a marriage ought to be.

Should I feel guilty, he had thought, *being so happy just now, so comforted?* And as if to compromise, he had indulged for a few days in what he came to see as a societally dictated grief. Grief. Yes, of course, he grieved, but in a sense of loneliness for Rick, not in hopeless sorrow.

For both him and Maggie, he sensed, Rick's death had closed the distance separating them from Beth and the children. Or, perhaps it wasn't actually their son's death that had prompted the change, but their own willingness to acknowledge Christian fellowship. Beth came often to Atlanta, and he and Maggie had spent several long weekends in Cleveland. When they were together, Pete's sibilant, gusty prayers and Justin's exuberant songs bridged the times between open tears. John could see that Rick had not left his sons emotional orphans. Now he recognized that his present happiness in the shadow of Rick's death came because he was himself no longer an emotional orphan. He had come home to God and God's people, and even when he went among strangers, he did so with a knowledge of his own paternity and the fact that he was never out of his Father's sight. On the other hand, John still felt off balance about the change in Maggie. Her openness almost embarrassed him after 30 years of his own clandestine Christianity. Perhaps even more surprising than her openness was the fresh way she looked at every spiritual dilemma. She was, he realized, not circumscribed by the pat terminology or predictable explanations that sometimes bound his own religious thought like adhesions clustering around an old incision, preventing natural flexing and stretching. She read for herself, and in her characteristically direct way, went straight to the heart of any issue she addressed, often with startling results. She attacked errors in her earlier opinions or in the opinions of others with the same insistence upon correctness that she demanded of a client's spreadsheet. Zero margin for errors. If God said it and the Holy Spirit led her to read it, she set about instant change.

John remembered walking in on a telephone conversation.

"That's not in the Bible, Corrine. It's coming from somewhere else. I don't want any part of it."

And her explanation when she hung up.

"Corrine thinks she's listening to Leighton's voice at her consciousness meetings. Leighton was only marginally reliable in the flesh. I wouldn't put full confidence in . . . John, if it really is his voice she hears now, that's not enough to give him credibility. I know I hear God's when I read the Bible."

She often brought out a Bible, its pages aflutter with slips of paper marking passages she had found, and interrogated him. Had he known this? Why hadn't he been doing what the Bible said about that?

Then one evening, throwing her arms around his neck, she burst into tears.

"I know, John, perfectly well why you've been compromising," she said. "Never again, John. Not for me."

At times he had wanted to sit down for whole days with her and unravel Bible doctrines as he understood them, but Maggie resisted.

"No, John. I've got to work this out without you. I've got to know I'm not just accepting an idea because that's what you think."

And so, while she cross-referenced, using the marginal

helps, and methodically charted her newly emerging beliefs in a notebook, John followed his key texts alone—those same key texts he had written in the margins of his Bible during his teen years when he hoped to use them to prove everything to Maggie and convert her. Now he knew he would have to tear loose the adhesions that had bound his own thinking, the same few references always attached to a predetermined conclusion as if the Bible were not an organic whole, each word and phrase related to every other word and phrase like tendons and nerves and muscles and bones, all feeding off the same blood supply and responding to the same brain. Even if the conclusion was correct, he realized, the connections had lost significance for him. He needed to open his Bible wider and allow the Holy Spirit to cut through the dead tissues of his thinking. If he wanted to keep pace with Maggie, he needed this kind of change.

John was unprepared for the green piano, already in place at the foot of the stairs when he walked through the foyer at home the next day. The room suddenly seemed a background in a painting composed expressly to house the piano. His lips were shaping an exclamation when Maggie, overtaking him in the hall, clapped her hand over his mouth.

"Play it, John."

She ran ahead of him to uncover the keyboard, then thumped the piano bench with her hand. "I know where your music is," she said, disappearing.

He played from memory until she returned from the basement with an armful of music books, delighting in the touch of the keys, the response of the total instrument.

"You're right, Maggie," he admitted after an hour. "At least Debussy sounds much better on a green piano."

Sitting on the bench next to him, her posture was as rigid as a 9-year-old about to play in her first recital. "Do you suppose," she said, "that God is more pleased if we pray in somber grays than if we come jubilant in purple and scarlet? Oh, John, I want a heaven resplendent with French horns and flutes. I could give up the 'rings on my fingers and bells on my toes' for a solid gold French horn and a green piano."

He glanced at her hands clasped across her skirt and caught her looking at the emerald set in silver on the finger next to her wedding band.

"Just—well, why?" she began.

"I don't know," he said.

"Sometimes I see why you believe the way you do, and sometimes, even reading the Bible—willing to accept anything God shows me there—I can't see at all. I mean, is God more pleased for the children to sing with a flea market piano without even a damp-chaser?"

He knew she was not really talking now about a piano—of whatever color or vintage.

John gathered the music together and reached to close the keyboard. "I've always thought of it in terms of an opportunity cost," he said.

"A trade-off for what?"

Slowly he ran his hand over the smooth green surface. "Maybe x-ray equipment or an airplane for a hospital in a developing country."

"I can't see it that way," Maggie said. "I'm sorry. I don't."

* * * *

In church a few days later Maggie remembered that conversation. Maybe the kids should have had the green piano. Was that what John meant? She glanced at the emerald on her middle finger. Just what was its opportunity cost? Almost a modest church if she could trust the figure quoted in the Mission Spotlight she had just seen. And what about her brass collection? The display cases alone—without a calculator she arrived at a total equal to a basic library for a school in one of John's developing nations. She wouldn't think about it now. Later when she could be objective.

* * * *

Lora sounded nonplused when John answered the phone on Sunday morning, as if she had expected her mother to answer and would rather not talk to him.

He told Lora about the piano.

"That's just like mother," she said, laughing. But her laugh was brittle.

"It sounds great, almost as good as it ought to for the price. Of course, I can only guess the price. Your mother makes sure I don't know all the details about some . . ."

"The preliminary hearing is Tuesday," Lora interrupted.

"Good. It will be a relief to get on with this business and get it over with."

"It's not that simple. Not that certain."

When she paused he didn't know what to say. He heard her blowing her nose and then drawing in her breath, slowly, deeply, to regain control of herself.

"It seemed simple, but it isn't. Some of the assumptions people used to make about child custody no longer apply. My lawyer has warned me to expect a rough battle. I wanted you and Mother to know about the hearing and that it might not turn out in my favor. I just wanted to know you were both behind me, thinking about me—with moral support."

"We'll be praying for you, too," her father said.

He could hear the half sob catch before she responded. "Don't. It didn't help Rick, and it won't help me."

* * * *

Maggie resumed her mental conflict while she walked the mall that morning. Halfway up the escalator she admitted to herself that she was in the habit of sacrificing many things in order to achieve her goals. All her life she had been accustomed to setting priorities and subordinating every other consideration in order to reach her objectives. Whether in business or her personal life.

She stepped off the escalator and established her stride before allowing her mind to proceed.

For example—

John's life before Rick's. If John had been the only match for the bone marrow transplant—No! She would never consent to even a small risk to her husband—not with his diabetes.

Every choice costs something, she thought, swallowing the rush of pain in her throat. Rick would have died even if John had been the donor. That wasn't the issue.

A young salesman turned from his shoe display. "Good morning," he said.

"Good morning," Maggie returned without pausing.

Everything has its price, she thought. And then she began to think of what her present peace—the certainty of forgiveness, the rest, the stillness at the center of her soul—what all this had cost God. *So far I haven't given up a thing. He's put everything at risk for my salvation. Does He expect me to start sacrificing some of my possessions—certainly not as payoffs—but just to be conducting my business the way He does His?* She took the elevator down and stopped, her hands resting on the ceramic rim of the fountain.

Her hands were thin like Granny's, her knuckles even more prominent, she noticed, as she turned the emerald solitaire halfway around her finger. The stone caught light reflected from the fountain, and for a moment the green was a rainbow widening from its own greenness to purple and gold.

* * * *

Lora looked at her nails, suddenly aware that she had been systematically chipping the dark red polish from the middle finger. Not only was the polish nearly gone, the nail itself was ragged where she had bit it. She felt a rush of panic. For a moment she was 10 again, facing her mother about chewing her nails.

"You lack self-control," her mother had said. "Or maybe it's self-esteem you lack. You lack something, Lora. Don't bite your nails. Not ever again."

"Yes, ma'am," Lora remembered saying.

Now she grasped the hand in the other, covering the evidence of her fall from grace. She forced her hands to stop trembling. *Will power*, she thought. *Self control.*

Why had she come early? *Why do I always arrive early?* She heard the judge talking with the two lawyers in a room to the right. Recognizing Rodnel's step in the hallway, she resisted the urge to turn as he entered the hearing room.

"Hello, Rodnel," she said when he sat down.

He did not answer.

"Why don't you want me to have Evyn?" she asked finally. "I can't believe you really want to bother with her yourself." Nervously she rubbed the rough fingernail with her other fingertips.

Rodnel pushed his chair back from the table. "Do you really want to know?"

"I asked."

He gripped the chair's armrests. "Because I don't want Evyn to have to bargain for any love she gets. I don't want her to get small amounts of love the way you'd give a kid a lollipop for good behavior. You're that way, Lora. You can't help it."

"She's my baby. I can't help loving her. I'll always love her." Lora felt her voice choke off.

"Sure, you'll love her—as long as she's flawless. She'll have to contract with you. If she meets your specifications, you'll reward her with a suitable amount of love in return. You'll measure it out in small enough installments that she'll always need more than she gets. You'll always make sure the 'goods' are delivered before you pay up. I got tired of buying you, Lora. I don't want my little girl to grow up that way."

"I'm not that way," she whispered. "I never was that way!"

* * * *

When he awoke Tuesday, John stretched twice out of habit, and then again out of habit, began to pray, first for Maggie, then for Rick's family, and finally for Lora. Halfway through the refrain about her success and safety, almost into the part about her responsibilities as a mother, he caught himself. The hearings were today.

"No, Lord, none of that perfunctory stuff. You know exactly what Lora's going through right now, and what kinds of resources she's going to need today. I don't have any suggestions. I can't tell You what to do for her."

Then he remembered that his daughter had forbidden him to pray for her. *As if I could help it*, he thought. *Besides, she was wrong about my prayers for Rick.*

"Lord, You didn't need Maggie's permission. When I asked, You changed her . . . touched her . . ."

Turning over, he rested his hand on Maggie's shoulder. She drew one quick breath, the way a child does when you pull the blanket up on a chilly morning.

"Now Lora, too, Lord. I know she's not a child any more, and I can't sign her permission slips the way I did when her class went to the zoo or the museum or even the release when she needed a tonsillectomy. But I'm still her dad. And I'm giving my permission. Go ahead in spite of what she says. Go ahead and help her."

* * * *

When Maggie glanced at the clock on her office wall at 10:00 a.m., she thought again about Lora and Rodnel and Evyn. By noon Lora would call her. Or maybe not if the hearing took longer than the half hour the lawyer had predicted.

Maggie reached for her phone and touched Memo 2. She listened to Lora's apartment phone ringing five, six times. Of course, she was already en route to the courthouse.

Switching to line 1, she waited for the phone to ring in her outer office.

"I'm expecting an important call from my daughter," she told her secretary. "Regardless of the transaction I'm in, let me know."

* * * *

At a quarter past one Lora followed her lawyer into an anteroom, feeling drained from the hearing. She had tried so desperately to establish her fitness as a mother—her financial competence, her stability, her good judgment.

The lawyer inserted his hand into his briefcase, making space for the folder before slipping it in.

"What you really are doesn't matter here, Lora. It's what Rodnel thinks you are—what the judge perceives you to be—ultimately—that matters. Remember Aristotle's rhetorical devices? Logos. Pathos. Ethos. You can reason and cry, but what you're up against is credibility."

Lora watched him snap his briefcase shut.

"And he can always argue that my two previous husbands would agree with him. That's the way they perceived me too. But I have been consciously working on it. I've been trying to relax—be more responsive to Evyn."

Dropping into a folding chair near the door, she told him about taking Evyn to work with her, to the park, letting work slide so they could be together.

"Why don't you just tell the judge that?" the lawyer suggested. "He's human. And he can always question your secretary or the day-care people if he wants corroboration."

"It's still scary," Lora replied. "I mean, no matter how much I try to change, I still feel pretty sure Rodnel is right— Bob and Carl too, probably."

"Don't keep putting yourself down," the lawyer said. He opened the door for her. "You could try behavior modification if you really want to make some basic personality changes."

Lora stepped into the nearly empty hallway. "That's the same system Rodnel predicted I'd use on Evyn. What I need is a fresh start with different genes and different primal instincts." She laughed but felt totally hopeless.

"My mother's a Southern Baptist," the lawyer said. "She'd call that a 'new birth.' "

She reached for the elevator button. "My dad's not a Baptist, but he'd use the same terminology."

* * * *

Lora looked at the books on the bedside table. The marker was in the paperback where she had put it before Rick died. She realized now that things would never be the same for her again. Somehow it was hard to sort out just what had happened. It wasn't just that her brother had died, but that at last she had seen that she could not really control very many things—not even her own emotions. Picking up the paperback, she opened it and glanced down the passage she had underlined, thinking how at the time she read it she had thought that it held the answer to her problems. Now she knew it did not.

I can never change myself—can never be anyone else or even a different me. I can't escape from who I've been and who I've become. I'm my mother's daughter.

Always washing. Mom and I are always washing, sweeping, organizing, displaying. We're clean, our houses and our lives are in order. We're poised. We're good!

But while my lovers ran away, tried to escape, Dad just loved Mom more for all her faults. Why?

Dropping the book to the floor, she reached to turn out the light, then lay in the darkness staring at the ceiling. *Certainly Dad wouldn't define the word exactly as it had been when she prepared to enter the Catholic Church, but it probably came down to the same thing—grace. Goodness that overflowed from somewhere—maybe from God—to nourish a human goodness that walked humbly and knew its own weakness.*

Rick had had that kind of grace. And even Justin and Pete understood it, she thought. *Dad had it, although he had subverted it at times. And Mom was beginning to see . . .*

"I want it too!" Lora said aloud and was startled by the loudness of her voice.

She wasn't certain about the appropriate way to approach God in her current confusion. Should she come as the Catholic she had become as an adult or as the divided child she had once been, torn between the two faiths her parents had seemed to reject. Precisely how did one pray to be born again?

As a child, of course, or however one could. "Wait for me, Daddy, I'm coming." Lora saw herself a dozen times over, always deciding after Rick and her father were already in the car that she wanted to go too, no matter where they were going. She saw herself flying down the front steps, still buttoning her coat, afraid they would leave without her.

And now, in the only way she could, she cried out to heaven.

"I'm coming."